THE INCREDIBLE MR SWEETS

OTHER WORKS

Concealed Words & Life – Life is a Culmination of Stories (Anthologies)

Shahenshah – Story of Shrenik Shah, the cancer conqueror

The Metro-Maniac Chronicles - Through the Eyes of an Obsessive-Compulsive Metro-Maniac

Double One Zero (110) – Out of the Shadows

Diary from Heaven - Confessions of an Eternal Junkie

Version One and a Half (Version 1 ½) - A glimpse of India in the '80s

JASVEER SINGH DANGI

THE INCREDIBLE MR SWEETS

THE COMING-OF-AGE STORY OF AN EX-CON WHO FINDS HIS CALLING IN LIFE THROUGH MUSIC

WWW.JASVEERSINGHDANGI.COM

Toronto

THE INCREDIBLE MR SWEETS – THE COMING-OF-AGE STORY OF AN EX-CON WHO FINDS HIS CALLING IN LIFE THROUGH MUSIC

ISBN - 978-1-7777253-3-4

‘The Incredible Mr Sweets – The coming-of-age story of an ex-con who finds his calling in life through music,’ is dedicated to my friend and business partner, Chetan Singh. He succumbed to Covid-19 on May 01, 2021, and this book wouldn’t have been complete without his continued support. Together, we started The Cog Publication LLP, India, to help aspiring authors publish their work. He was a dreamer, a great storyteller, and a published author himself. He wanted to help aspiring authors with any support they needed.

Chetan was the kind of person who would go out of the way to help people. As a lawyer, he helped many by working for free, and as a Political Analyst, he raised relevant issues on television without any fear or pressure.

His caring nature, continuous encouragement and smile are what I am going to miss the most. Miss you, my friend and brother from another mother. May God bless your soul.

RIP MY DEAR FRIEND

Talent-based reality shows are a great way to showcase your talent in front of a vast audience. Every country has its version of such reality shows. This book is dedicated to the countless talented seniors who have appeared on reality shows across the world.

Some of them practised their talent: such as singing, dancing, comedy, etc., for many years but never made it big, so they appeared in talent shows to prove to the world that they are worth it. Some could never pursue what they loved because of monetary reasons and were stuck doing something else to earn a living. Others never dared to showcase their talent in public, while the rest only came to know about their talent quite late, so they wanted to showcase their talent at this stage in life. Whatever be the reason, they have all dazzled the world with their brilliant performances through many reality shows.

Ray Jessel (God bless his soul) - 84 years, Nora Barton - 96 years, Frank Dimitri - 74 years, Janey Cutler - 80 years, Evelyn Williams - 81 years, Sarah Patricia Jones popularly known as Paddy Jones - 86 years, Josefina Monasterio - 73 years, Marty Ross - 80 years, and countless others are truly amazing. The list is endless, and I wish I could name them all. They all prove that it's never too late to learn or start something new.

Even age couldn't diminish their passion for their respective talent, and they performed in front of massive audience across the world effortlessly. Some of them used reality shows to showcase their talents, while others chose digital media to bring their talent to the world. Digital media has opened a lot of avenues for people to showcase their talent.

'The Incredible Mr Sweets - The coming-of-age story of an ex-con who finds his calling in life through music,' is a salute to such brave hearts.

DISCLAIMER

'The Incredible Mr Sweets – The coming-of-age story of an ex-con who finds his calling in life through music,' is a work of fiction. Names, characters, ethnicities, businesses, brands, events, and incidents depict a fictional story. Reference to places, brands, songs, movies and movie characters has only been used for storytelling purposes. Though inspired by a real-life show, reference to a reality show format is not meant to disrespect any show or a person in any way. Prison procedures referred to in the story are based upon research, and the author doesn't claim that they are 100% accurate.

'I have come too far,' has been penned by Pranay Sharma and, 'There's a place far away,' has been composed by Kavita Kabira, aka Kavita Bhutani especially for 'The Incredible Mr Sweets' and Jasveer Singh Dangi holds the copyright for these.

I have included many of my favourite classic song titles in the story. I hope you will enjoy them as well, as much as I enjoy listening to them. Copyright for these song titles used for storytelling purpose belong to the respective copyright owners: "My way" by Frank Sinatra, "Eight days a week" by the Beatles, "Mei Jatt Yamla Pagla Deewana" by Mohammed Rafi, "Ajj Din Chadiya" by Rahat Fateh Ali Khan, "Concrete heart" by Great Lakes Swimmers, "I am a woman" by Helen Reddy, "A Natural Woman" by Aretha Franklin, "You Don't mess around with Jim" by Jim Croce, "Lady in Red" by Chris De Burgh, "Wonderful Tonight" by Eric Clapton, "Can't take my eyes off you" by Frankie Valli and the 4 Seasons, "Ain't no sunshine when she's gone" by Bill Withers, "Swinging on a Star" by Bing Crosby.

ABOUT JASVEER

Jasveer is an author, podcast host, behavioural trainer and award-winning health and safety professional. He is currently based in Canada. He was part of the team of trainers that trained 22,000 volunteers for the Commonwealth Games 2010 in New Delhi.

Awards & Recognition:

1. Rated as one of the 10 Indian Authors Redefining Modern Literature by Kathmandu Tribune in Jan 2020.
2. Recognized by Ne8X with Sahitya Kosh Samman Award in Literature.
3. In 2018, he was awarded by IISSM for his contributions towards the Health and Safety Training domain.
4. In 2019, Literature Light recognized him as top 100 debut authors for his debut book Version One and a Half (Version 1 ½).
5. He was named as the 'Author of the Fest' at the Writing Wizards Fest 2020 for his book Double One Zero (110) - Out of the shadows. The Writing Wizards Fest is an initiative by The Twilight of Poem www.twilightofpoem.in.

He loves the outdoors and is a big movie buff, which is quite evident given the use of quotes and songs from movies at strategic places in all his books. He is an avid observer of his surroundings and uses characters and instances from everyday situations for his stories. He has published five books and co-authored two anthologies so far.

He also shares his thoughts on www.storymirror.com, www.medium.com, www.merrative.com, www.theceylonvoice.com, www.socialist-today.com, #jasveersinghdangi (Instagram account and his Facebook page). He is actively engaged in helping budding authors through articles, seminars, and workshops. He also hosts a podcast; interviewing authors and other professionals on his website www.jasveersinghdangi.com.

CONTENTS

THE INCREDIBLE MR SWEETS

'Better late than never'

The effects of lockdown are not even closer to what a prisoner feels while being incarcerated for a long time in prison, but lockdown gave me the idea for this book. Though the never-ending lockdown for me, starting in India and then in Canada, has been uncomfortable, it is necessary to stop the spread of the Covid-19 virus. The lockdown got me thinking about the psychology of a prisoner who has been in prison forever and the mix of emotions he would experience after being released. This ideation led me to 'The Incredible Mr Sweets'.

So, what goes through the mind of a hardened criminal when he is released from prison after thirty-four years?

A mix of emotions ranging from happiness and excitement of being free to confusion and maybe even fear of unwelcome society's wrath and people not accepting him. He might also feel lost because the world would've changed so much by the time he comes out of prison. This could all happen to anyone but not John Sweets Russo. He's a tough nut to crack, and thirty-four years in prison couldn't break his spirit. Though he came out of the prison burdened with guilt, he was ready to face the world head-on. He will not let his guilt bend him down and let the world break his spirit. He is not asking for a second chance from anyone. He is making a come-back.

John Sweets Russo was once the left-hand man of William Vallery, the head of the notorious Vallery gang of Toronto and now aspires to be a singer. He is looking for a chance to make the most of his life that is left, considering he is seventy-five now. As he got out of prison and joined a world he didn't recognize anymore, all he wanted to do was to sing.

'The Incredible Mr Sweets' is the coming-of-age story that chronicles an ex-con's journey to becoming a singing star.

‘The Incredible Mr Sweets’ also highlights the identity crisis faced by immigrant’s children born in Canada.

Life’s all about making the best of what you have before you aspire for something else.

Did you make the most out of what you had?

Are you making the most out of what you have?

Very few people get a second chance in life like Jasmeet John Sweets Russo. Even after making some horrible decisions in life, he gets a second chance. Not many are as lucky as he is. **Make the most of what you have**.

Bullying and racial prejudice in all forms must be condemned and stopped. Canada is a country created by an amalgamation of various cultures, with every culture given equal importance.

"The world needs more Canada." Bono

FREEDOM

The sheer magnitude of emotions that a person goes through can be overwhelming when released from a small prison cell after a long time. John Russo was no different. He, too, had the same anxiety, and his mind was clouded with millions of doubts as the day of his release came closer. Ever since John was informed that he was being pardoned and that he would be released six years earlier than his actual release date, he had been going through varied emotions. But, he had been preparing for his release for a long time. John had made up his mind to make the most of his life left once he was released. Unlike the other aged prisoners, he didn't want to just go out and retire to an old age home; John wanted to make his parents proud. He wanted to achieve something. So, the fact that the day came six years earlier had sort of subsided every negative emotion and nervousness in him and made him happy instead. John looked forward to his second chance.

John was reading the quotation on the piece of paper his mother had given him. It was a Shabad (Verse) from Guru Granth Sahib Ji. His mother had given it to him when she came to meet him after he was convicted. It was written in Punjabi. John had been in prison for a long-time, and that piece of paper was all he had to remember his mother and God almighty. John read it every day without fail.

It read, *"God is celebrated and acclaimed all over the world; it is fruitful and rewarding to serve Him. Lofty, infinite, and immeasurable is the Lord; all beings are in His Hands. Nanak has entered the Sanctuary of God; He is with me everywhere. His circle of protection is our life. Therefore, relieving the stress and anxiety of modern living and bringing calmness and serenity in life."*

**On 'Ang (Para) 819' of Sri Guru Granth Sahib Ji, this divine "Taati Wao Na Lagai Shabad (Verse)" was written by Guru Arjan Dev Ji. This Shabad is known to protect* *one's mind and body, bringing His circle of protection into our life.*

'EXCITED?' Loud Joe asked in his usual high volume.

John was sitting on the lower bed in his prison cell reading the Shabad. Loud Joe was standing outside the cell with a broom, and the cell door was open for cleaning. John folded the paper, kept it on the bed, and looked up, took off his glasses and found Loud Joe smiling at him; he smiled back. John was being pardoned and was being released early because of his excellent behaviour and age.

'I guess so. I am getting out of here today.' John said as he got up to hug Loud Joe. John then adjusts the earpiece of Loud Joe's hearing aid. 'Better,' John says, smiling.

The earpiece of Loud Joe's hearing aid mostly slipped out of his ear without him realising it.

Loud Joe had been there for a long time as well. He had lost his right ear to a prison fight earlier, while diabetes slowly took away the hearing in his left ear. Everyone loved Loud Joe because he was their go-between for anything they wanted in prison. He did many odd jobs, including stacking books in the prison library and cleaning. John was an avid reader, and Loud Joe was his saviour. Loud Joe would provide him with the latest books to read. He could also get the small things done for the prisoners, and the guards usually ignored it because he was Loud Joe, after all. Loud Joe was a smooth talker, and he could get his way with the guards.

'I am gonna miss your voice, Sweets, and so will everyone else in this block,' Loud Joe said as he got emotional. John was nicknamed Sweets and was known as John Sweets Russo in his circle. He had a powerful voice and was loved for his singing skills.

'Now you don't get emotional for me, you fool.' John said, tickling Loud Joe.

'I am really gonna miss you, Sweets,' Loud Joe said.

John sees Loud Joe lowering his head in disappointment. He whistles, and that immediately puts a huge smile on Loud Joe's face. John firstly hummed along with Loud Joe and then sang the song a cellmate had written for him. His voice could lighten up any grim situation in prison.

'I have come too far; I want to get back to where it all starts...

There was a line people fear to cross, a destiny they can't dare to choose...'

His voice resonated in the cell and created some good old vibes. John then started whistling as Loud Joe continued the song along with others in the neighbouring cells.

'But I somehow managed to climb up the hills.

Yes, I chased my dreams... I miss the smell of that lily, I miss my mom's gift of that li'l car...'

John stopped whistling and joined them.

'I have come too far, I have come too far & now....'

Suddenly, he stopped singing as he felt a huge lump in his throat. He swallowed. There was silence in the block as the sound of his hiccuped voice made everyone emotional. Then a weak voice came from the corner.

'Wanna get back to where it all starts...' guard Simon walked in singing. This song was quite popular with everyone around, and John would sing it often.

'This block will be quite dull after you are gone, Sweets,' Simon said as John looked smiling.

John had two things going for him in there; that quote in his pocket and the singing. Every chance he got to sing, he would do that with full enthusiasm. Many prisoners came and went out in that block, but everyone remembered Sweets for his fantastic voice.

*****

John's real name was Jasmeet Singh Brar, a name he had long forgotten, a name he had given up, despite opposition from his parents because he wanted to feel and look just like a Canadian. Even as per the prison records, his name was John Russo.

His parents had migrated to Canada from Punjab, India, in the early 1930s for a better future, and John was born here on December 23, 1938. Since childhood, he was groomed by his father to recite Shabad Gurbani *(Shabad is a word meaning hymn, sacred song, sound, verse, voice, or word. The Shabad's or hymns of Guru Granth Sahib are known as Gurbani or the Guru's word and are written in the Gurmukhi script and composed in Raag, a musical score)*.

John grew up in Brampton in the Greater Toronto Area. His parents raised him with Sikh beliefs, but his beliefs were shaken up by constant bullying in school.

He had grown up facing bullying in his school for his Sikh lineage. Like many other immigrants, he too picked up an English alias to fit in. He would introduce himself as John instead of Jasmeet, and rather than reciting what his father wanted, he would sing English songs. This was his way of finding a place in a predominantly white crowd in the school those days. While his singing was quite popular in the school, bullying still didn't stop.

Initially, he would just introduce himself as John and then changed his name officially when he turned eighteen, much to his father's discomfort. He became John Brar, formally. He also gave up his kesh (hair) and the turban to even look like a Canadian at twenty-one. He walked out of the house that day after a huge argument with his father.

He had struggled with a sandwiched identity between his Sikh lineage and the Canadian culture, where he was born and raised throughout his childhood.

After leaving his family house in 1959, he moved to the St. James town neighbourhood in Downtown Toronto. He lived in a plain old-fashioned house, sharing a room with five others. That is where he met his friend Samuel. A nice Italian lady owned the place.

John hummed a tune as Samuel sat on the porch outside their house, sipping beer.

'I want to change my last name as well,' John said. It was a late night, and the neighbourhood was quiet.

Samuel thought for a moment as he walked around. John looked on.

'STOP LOITERING AROUND SO LATE; PEOPLE ARE TRYING TO SLEEP,' the landlady screamed from the window upstairs.

John and Samuel looked up, sending flying kisses her way.

'We love you, Mrs Russo,' John and Samuel said together.

Mrs Russo closed the window, mumbling a few words angrily. She knew that they both were incorrigible. Samuel and John laugh.

Samuel suddenly stops laughing and smiles while looking at John. John stops laughing, seeing Samuel smile.

'What?' John asked, looking at Samuel's weird smile.

'How about Russo? John Russo?' he said and looked at John.

'Russo? That's Italian,' John said and thought.

'It means red,' Samuel said and looked at John, smiling.

'Red hot John,' Samuel said, giggling as he referred to John's hot temper.

John takes out a picture of his parents from his wallet. 'No going back.' He places the picture back in his wallet.

'John Russo it is,' John said, raising his bottle.

'Cent' Anni… JOHN RUSSO!' Samuel said, raising his bottle.

'Cent' Anni *(May you live hundred years)*!' John exclaimed.

From that time onwards, no one ever called him John Brar; he was always known as John Russo, which would give him infamy. With his fair skin and Canadian accent, he did look and sound like a 'John Russo'. The neighbourhood had many hard-working Italians, and John also learned the basic Italian language while living there.

Samuel got them a job at a warehouse. They would work through the night in the warehouse and then also did part-time work during the daytime. John would take time out for plays and auditions as well. They worked hard to make ends meet. They were earning decent money but not enough to live a lavish life, and this was when they hooked up with a local gang involved in petty theft and other small-time crimes for some easy money. That was when they were led towards their first encounter with the law when they both were arrested. They hooked up with William Vallery in prison.

While John moved ahead in the crime world and became rich, he never forgot the neighbourhood. He helped many people with jobs and money. Despite his notoriety as a gangster, he was well respected in the community.

*****

John hands over the books to Loud Joe, and Joe hugs him with moist eyes. John was also getting emotional, but he hides his tears.

John looks around the cell and takes off some old newspaper cuttings pasted on the wall. He looks at his parent's old photograph, almost choking on emotions. He packs his stuff in a box and gets ready to leave his cell after thirty-four years. He walks out carrying his box. The inmates in the other cells stood up to pay respect to John Sweets Russo. Everyone respected John. No one bothered him, and all the years he was here, he never bothered anyone.

'Hey, Sweets, if you ever need anything after getting out, get in touch with my cousin Autumn in Toronto. He is well connected,' a prisoner said, passing a piece of paper. John looks at the guard, who nods in approval, and then John takes the paper slip and keeps it in his box.

'Ciao, Sweets,' the man said.

'Ciao,' John replies.

John is then taken to the administration block for some paperwork and his belongings.

'It's been an honour knowing you, Mr Russo,' said Kalm, who had been the Jailer of the Delimit Institution for over fifteen years. Like everyone else, he, too, was a big fan of John's fantastic voice.

'Thank you,' John says. He was trying hard to put up a brave front and not show emotions.

John looked through his belongings kept on the table with nostalgia. He looked at his watch. It was a 1972 Audemars Piguet, and he remembered the time it was gifted to him by none other than the famous singer and actor Claudio Romano at an after-show party.

*****

It was January 1974, and Claudio had performed at the Desert Inn Palace Casino in Las Vegas. He and a couple of his close friends enjoyed the after-party in the early morning hours along with John's boss.

The Vallery gang operated in Toronto, Montreal, and other parts of Canada and had business interests in the USA as well. A regular patron at the Desert Inn Palace Casino, John's boss, William, also had close contacts with many mob families in the USA.

'Heard that you are a good singer?' Claudio asked John, who, as usual, stood there silently.

'John's a great singer,' John's boss William said.

Claudio was drunk. He got up and walked in an unsteady gait towards John, who had his eyes covered with dark sunglasses. Claudio removed John's glasses and looked at him closely. He kisses John on both his cheeks and then takes off his watch and slides it on John's arm. He kisses John again.

'Hey, bring us some drinks,' Claudio said as his equally drunk friend brought him two shots. He gave one shot to John and the other to Claudio.

'Cheers,' said Claudio.

*****

The sound of glasses hitting together echoed in John's ears as he wore the watch again after so many years.

*****

Once John finished his drink, Claudio hugged him. The moment he hugged John, Claudio could feel something under his jacket. Claudio looked down and saw the gun holster visible.

'He's very creative with that as well,' William said, pointing towards the gun. Claudio was so drunk that he didn't even hear what William said. Claudio simply walked back to the table.

'Hey, sing something for us,' Claudio said, coming back to his chair and looking back, but John remained quiet.

'Don't be shy, John, it's just us here,' Claudio said, looking around at all the empty tables. John's boss had booked the place for the singer and his entourage.

'Go on, John,' William said.

John cleared his throat and sang a few lines of 'Bella Ciao (Goodbye beautiful),' and Claudio clapped, getting up. He again rushed towards John and kissed him.

'He's got a sweet voice. He's Johnny Sweets,' Claudio said.

'JOHNNY SWEETS,' everyone said together, raising their glasses, and the name stuck with John forever. Claudio wasn't the first one to refer to John as Sweets.

While everyone enjoyed their drinks, John looked distraught and walked out of the room. The word 'Sweets' sent him on a whirlwind ride of memories as this was the name given to him by his mother.

A man sees John coming out and firstly waves at him outside the hall and then says, 'Hello John.' John simply walks away, ignoring the man. John was feeling uncomfortable.

John rushed out of the building into the parking lot, where he stood alone staring at the sky. It had become difficult for John to visit Brampton without drawing attention from law enforcement agencies, so he hadn't visited the place for many years. He stood there, visualising his mother referring to him as Sweets.

*****

John smiles, remembering about the night. He took off the watch and left it on the table.

Amongst his other belongings was a Borsalino Brown Fedora hat, something he was very fond of during his days of notoriety. Seeing the hat brought back visuals of his notorious past as a gangster, and he kept the hat back on the table as well.

'I don't need anything,' he said, leaving his belongings there. He only carried the box from his cell with him. He also changed his prison clothes, and for the first time in so many years, he was wearing something other than the standard clothes for prisoners.

Being in prison for such a long time, he was given clothes made by prisoners because he didn't want to wear any of his old clothes. Typically, clothes are brought by relatives or people known to prisoners upon their release. But John had barred his family from meeting him. So, no one even knew that he was being released today. His actual prison sentence was to end in 2020.

John was given a debit card for an account where all his earnings in prison were deposited, along with contact details for resources such as housing facilities, counsellor etc., which he could use if he needed assistance. Since he was pardoned, he wasn't required to report to anyone after his release.

As he is given the final go-ahead to leave, John feels like he left his old body and entered a new body altogether. John walked out of the administration office with confidence, and he moves towards the main exit.

As he signed in the register kept on the table outside the guard's cabin near the main gate, he looked at his reflection in the glass window and saw his wrinkled face and grey hair. He smiled and realised that he wasn't the same man as he was thirty-four years ago, after all. His calmness vanished instantly, and he felt nervous. He looked at the main gate with a subtle uneasiness. He carried his box and paced towards the gate.

'You will be alright, John. You are still the same,' he thought, trying to motivate himself. He smiles though he was nervous. 'Congratulations, John, you are free again.' He mumbled as he gets closer to the gate.

As he walked, he visualised his younger self walking in, and as they were about to cross each other, the younger John stopped and held the older John's hand and said, 'Don't screw it up this time,' and the younger self walked inside the prison.

'John,' he heard someone call his name and turned around towards the main gate. Guard Roger was calling his name. He looked around and found that younger John was no longer there.

'Wassup Sweets, you getting cold feet about going back to the outside world?' Roger asked as John reached the main gate.

'No, not at all. I am super excited to get out,' John replied.

'All right, you have a good one,' Roger said, bringing his knuckle out, and John brought his knuckle forward as well. John gave a faint smile as they bumped knuckles.

*****

John Russo was the name synonymous with terror when he was a part of the Vallery gang. He worked for the gang for many years until a rival killed his boss, and John got arrested in Toronto. His friend and brother, from another mother, Samuel, was also killed on the same day. John was also shot in his arm and leg and was captured while he was on anaesthesia during surgery. By the time he woke up at the hospital, the doctor had informed the cops, and he was already in cuffs.

It took him a few weeks to recover in the hospital, and then he was shifted to prison and had been there ever since, after his conviction. He blamed himself for Samuel and his boss's murder. But when five men rain bullets, then you alone cannot do much. Seeing William and Samuel getting killed in front of him had left John devastated, and then seeing his parents in the court every time further added to the emotional chaos. The very family he had left years ago was back, standing with him and supporting him when he felt he had lost everything. His life flashed in front of him as he would sit in the court while the lawyers argued. No matter how much he tried to avoid it, he would always end up looking at his old parents sitting amidst the crowd in the courtroom.

John was remorseful, and he wanted to confess everything, but William's widow, Bella, had convinced John not to share anything about the gang and the business. John confessed to committing the crimes on his own. Bella had hired good lawyers for John. Minus any link to the gang, John's confession had gotten him forty years in the maximum-security prison. He kept his word and never mentioned the Vallery gang ever.

John’s reputation from outside preceded him inside the prison as well; everyone respected him. Everyone knew that John was caught while he was injured and unconscious and the fact that he never ratted out gave him a rock star status in prison.

Singing in prison started as a stress buster initially, and then his voice mesmerised everyone around, so he started doing it regularly. John wanted to become a singer and an actor since childhood. He would audition for voiceover assignments when he was still in school. John's mother had always encouraged his singing talent, even as his father didn't like John singing anything but Shabad Gurbani. She called him 'Mittha (Sweet)' for two reasons: his sweet voice and his sweet tooth. John was fond of sweets, and his mother made many Indian sweets, Jalebi being his favourite, at home, especially for him.

He sounded just like any other Canadian those days, but every time he went for an audition, kids would make fun of his race, and that's why he wanted to sound and look like a Canadian. With every jab or comment about his Sikh looks, he got more and more angry and resentful. He didn't just want to look like them; he wanted to prove that he was better than those making fun of him. That turned out to be a big mistake, in fact, a monumental mistake that would later entangle him in a downward spiral of negativity and drag him away from his own identity.

He did a few small-time singing gigs and acted in plays at local theatres when he moved to Downtown Toronto but got caught up in the world of crime soon after. To make some quick money, he and Samuel initially committed petty crimes. They were arrested for arson and burglary, and it was in the prison where they met William Vallery, a small-time mobster in those days. They became close, and upon their release, they started working for him. John was filled with rage due to constant bullying, and this rage propelled him to the top in the Vallery gang. John took out his anger on anyone who opposed William.

Initially, William operated from the same neighbourhood, and then they spread their operations through Canada and the USA. John became crucial in his journey to finally reach Vegas and own a Casino. With John's support, William achieved notoriety, and the Vallery gang became increasingly influential.

Everyone knew about John and his temper. John could learn things quickly. He was a brilliant guy, and he could've done anything with his life if he wanted to, but he chose the life of a criminal instead. He was a feared gangster who had roughed up, shot, and seriously injured many people. Though he was known for his rage, he operated the gang shrewdly. He did his job with planning and precision, ensuring safety from cops. Cops could never link him or William to any murder or crime. John was the most powerful man and indirectly controlled the entire gang. John was always close to William when William lived and when he died right in front of John.

*****

April 28, 2014

As John left the prison gate, he felt nervous seeing the outside world after such a long-time. He looked around and saw no one waiting for him. It was the complete contrast of the time he was brought in here thirty-four years ago. The place was crawling with reporters and photographers, then trying to get something out of him when he walked into the prison gate after his conviction.

'No one?' he wondered, looking at the empty parking lot.

John realised that he had not contacted anyone in the neighbourhood while he was in prison, and his remaining family, too, had no idea that he was being released. The only regular visitor he had, except for his mother, was his lawyer, that too only for the first few years. During every visit, the lawyer reminded him against talking about the gang with the cops.

John felt horrible, and he had tried hard to dissuade his mother from visiting him. No matter how much John tried, his mother would not relent, and she would come to meet him regularly till she died.

'Just you, John,' he mumbled and took a deep breath.

He tried hard not to look back, but finally, he stopped walking, kept the box down, and turned around. His eyes got moist as the prison gate closed. He then turned around, whipping his eyes, walked towards the bus stop, and sat there on the bench. He came out at around 1:30 PM. Since he had been incarcerated for a long time, John had been briefed about the lifestyle outside before his release. John knew where to go and how to go, but he chose to sit there for a long time.

THE NERVOUS WRECK

Clearly, the anxiety of seeing the outside world after such a long time was overwhelmingly overshadowing the joy of being free. John was wary of getting close to people as he thought someone might recognise him. He was all over the newspapers when he was convicted. Every time someone passed the bench, he would look away, trying to hide his face.

He sat there for a while and then smiled and giggled. 'That was a long time ago, you moron. No one would recognise your wrinkled face now,' he mumbled and noticed that many people walked past him, and no one even looked at his face.

Even after realising the same, he just sat there looking at people. He was so used to the prison life that it took him some time to get out of the prison mode and realise that no one would order him to get up and talk to people. He was used to living without talking to anyone for hours. Everything he did in prison was part of a routine, and it was punishable to go against the routine there; he soon realised that he was no longer in prison.

Finally, he gathered some courage and nervously enquired about the time; it was already 3:40 PM. He had been sitting there all this while. Seeing the man smile while telling him the time gave John the necessary boost he needed. He asks the same man for directions. The person directed him to an ATM nearby. John withdraws some cash and then checks the route map at a transit stop. He was eagerly looking to visit his old neighbourhood in Toronto. Since it was already getting late, he decides to stay in a hotel for the night.

John strolled around and explored the area, looking for a hotel. He walked slower than everyone else — thirty-four years of ambling in a line in the prison sort of configured his body accordingly.

‘Sir, where can I find a cheap hotel?’ John politely asks a man coming out of an LCBO store. The man looks at John and smiles. He directs John to a hotel nearby.

It was a small hotel. John finds the hotel to his liking and checks in for the night. After the check-in, he comes out for a walk and tries to get used to the feeling of being free.

The feeling was a mixed one. While he was happy being released after such a long time and focused on the task at hand, he was nervous as well; will the world accept an ex-convict? Will they let him lead a normal life? Will he be able to find work?

‘Should I go to India?’ was another thought as he visualised his life walking around.

‘But I have never been to India,’ he thought, countering his earlier thought.

He was walking around aimlessly, lost in random thoughts, and soon reaches a park. He looks around and is happy to see the greenery all around. Though there were many plants and trees in prison as well, this was different. John walked closer to a tree and feels it with both his hands. He feels like a child who had just been reunited with his mother.

Since it was evening, many people were walking around the park, and kids were also playing. John suddenly noticed a couple of people staring at him, and he immediately looked away. He quickly sat on a park bench, hiding his face.

‘This is going to take some time,’ he thinks. He was feeling stupid about hiding his face from people again and again.

He breathes deep and closes his eyes for a moment enjoying the breeze. He visualises his mother taking him to the park for a walk. This calms him, and John slowly opens his eyes after some time. He sat in the garden, looking at the world.

‘One day at a time, John, take it nice and easy,’ he mumbled.

John notices that the world has changed a lot since he went to prison. Some things bewildered him while other changes were pleasant. While he couldn't understand why people kept staring at their phones even while walking in the park, he was happy to see several Asians and people of other ethnicities around.

He sat there enjoying the breeze, which he enjoyed a lot in prison as well when they could be in the open area, but the breeze today felt different. He tried concentrating on the pleasantness, but again and again, his brain would switch back to the crazy thoughts, and nervousness would kick in.

He felt like talking to people but was too nervous about what they would think if he shared that he had just gotten out of prison. These thoughts were overwhelming. His brain was again overworking with so many ideas. He didn't even realise that a soccer ball was lying close to his feet and a girl was screaming from a distance.

'CAN YOU PLEASE THROW THE BALL BACK?' she screamed as John sat there, oblivious to everything around him.

Seeing John not move, she rushes towards him.

'Are you all right, sir?' the girl asked, picking up the soccer ball. John breathed heavily and looked at her.

'Do you need some water?' the girl asked, passing her water bottle to John.

'I am, I am…,' John said and paused, trying to control his breathing.

'I am just out of breath,' he said, trying to put a smile on his face.

'If you need help, let me know. I will be over there,' she said, pointing towards other kids. John smiled, and she smiled back.

She got busy playing soccer with other kids. After about ten minutes, she looked back, but John was gone. She looked around to see if John might need help, but John was already on his way to the hotel by then.

He stayed in the room for the rest of the evening. All through the night, he kept tossing and turning in the bed, preparing an introductory script. He kept thinking about the ways to introduce himself and could not sleep all night.

The following day he checked out quite early and reached the bus stop, and left for Toronto. There were no direct buses to Toronto; he had to change multiple buses and reached Union Station Toronto at 12:30 PM.

As he enters the Great Hall of Union Station, nostalgia sets in. The Great Hall hadn't changed even a bit since John was here the last time. Barring a few changes, it still looked the same to him. John feels tired from the journey and sits in the Great Hall. As he sits there reminiscing of his dark past, amongst the ocean of people moving through the Great Hall, he hears a familiar sound and compulsively follows it.

His face lights up like a Christmas tree as he gets closer to the source of the sound. It was a kid playing the piano in the corner. The piano was placed there by a retail brand for promotions, and anybody could play it. He plays it masterfully, and his fingers move on the keyboard like a professional. John recognises the notes; it was "*Swinging on a Star*" by Bing Crosby.

John visualises his mother getting him a piano. His father wanted him to learn to play the harmonium or tabla (Indian musical instruments used in Gurudwara during prayers), but John wanted to learn piano. Despite opposition from his father, his mother saved money and got him a used piano.

John walks up to the piano and stands beside the kid. He was oblivious to John and the rest of the world. John starts humming the lyrics as he follows the tune, and the kid looks up smiling, hearing John's subtle humming. The kid points towards the mic, and John gets down and sits next to him. John gets closer to the mic and sings the melancholy tune, following the kid.

John sings joyfully as the kid plays, and the Great Hall echoes with the melodious sounds.

Many people gather around the piano, and they enjoy themselves as they both continue for some more time. Suddenly John notices people making videos on their phones and clicking pictures. He feels like he is in a time machine and was back outside the prison thirty-four years ago. John sees news reporters surrounding him wanting to know his story. He stops his singing and breathes heavily. He looks around, and for a moment, it is as if his ears are switched to silent mode, and he is about to pass out. John can't hear anything. Suddenly he feels a tap on his shoulder and looks around. A lady was saying something, but all John could see was her lips moving. The lady continues to speak, but John is not able to hear anything. John feels as if his heart is about to explode when he notices the kid touching his hand. The kid has the most adorable smile. John smiles back, and he starts hearing again.

'Thaaank youu,' the kid says, stammering a bit.

'You are welcome, you little genius,' John pats his face.

'Are you alright?' the lady asks, seeing John feeling uncomfortable.

'I am alright. Too much excitement, I guess,' John smiles. Finally, he gathers himself and comes back to his senses.

'Thank, you sir!' the lady says. She is the kid's mother.

'Clyde has Down syndrome, and the piano is all that keeps him focused. Anywhere he sees one, he has to play it. Thank you for joining him.' She smiles.

'Nice to meet you, Clyde; I am John,' John says, shaking hands with Clyde.

'You have a gifted child here. Make sure he continues playing because music is a powerful medium,' John says and left from there. As he leaves, he hears the sound of the piano and then again smiles.

John takes a subway, followed by a streetcar to St James Town. As he travels through the streetcar, he looks around.

Though there were many changes, he could still recognise some shops and landmarks.

The excitement to see the neighbourhood after so many years soon turns into nervousness, again, as John again starts avoiding anyone looking at him. He thinks someone might recognise him. John walks through the streets of St James Town slowly while avoiding anyone looking at him. It seems that this part of the neighbourhood hasn't changed much in the last thirty-four years; his memory has changed, though. It is indeed difficult for him to remember where he is supposed to go. He soon realises that he has no place to go.

Again, something that baffles him is that most people look into their phones rather than talking to each other. This is the startling difference between the '70s when he went to prison and now. No one is talking to each other; they only stare at their phones.

He walks around for a while and then spots River Bakery at a distance. He remembers when he had initially moved here, the neighbourhood kids would crowd the bakery in the early mornings, and the shop owner would give them soft Pignoli cookies. This was his favourite shop for candies and the best way to satisfy his urge for sweets.

Today he is walking into the same bakery; it is no longer a small neighbourhood shop of the '70s but an expensive-looking restaurant. He looks through the counter and realises that he had overcome his sweet tooth while in prison. He smiles and orders some Pignoli cookies and a bottle of water. From here, reaching his old house wasn't difficult for him. It is about nine hundred meters from the bakery.

It was an old house in an alley. It was here that his journey as John Russo started about fifty years ago. The house was owned by one of Samuel's aunts, and the rent was relatively minor. He and Samuel remained inseparable till Samuel's death.

As John looks at the porch of his old house, his mind is lit up with memories of his initial days here. He steps up onto the porch and lifts the carpet in the corner. He then slides the wood under it, and this reveals a secret compartment. He and Samuel would hide bottles of illegal liquor in this corner of the porch.

He knocks at the door and sits on the stairs. The stairs and the porch seem dirty. The scattered leaves on the floor show that the place hasn't been cleaned in a while. After some time, when no one opens the door, John gets up to leave.

'Can I help you? There's no one in that house,' John hears a voice and turns around. It was someone from the neighbouring house.

'I wanted to see Mrs Russo,' John says.

'Mrs Russo hasn't been around for a long time,' the man says, and John looks dejected.

'I haven't been here in a while, but I sort of hoped that she might still be around,' John says.

'Can I help you?' the man asks, and John looks at the house.

'Wasn't this house also owned by her family,' John asks, looking at the house.

'Yes, it still is,' the man says. 'Let me open the door. Come on in, you look thirsty,' he says.

John walks up to the door of the neighbouring house, and the door opens. It was an old man, probably older than John.

'Thank you,' John says, entering the house.

'I am Joel,' the man says, extending his hand.

'I am John.' John extends his hand, but Joel quickly pulls back his hand.

'You are John? John Russo?' Joel says with a touch of anger in his voice.

'Yes,' John replies calmly.

'I am Joel…' he says and looks at John. His eyes turn red with anger.

'I am sorry. I don't remember you,' John says.

'I am Kathleen Russo's brother, Joel Russo,' he says, and John is taken aback.

'Kathleen, ah… Mrs Russo died three years after you were caught,' Joel says with tears in his eyes.

'I had no idea about this; I am so sorry,' John says remorsefully.

'Doesn't matter now. She went through hell after you and Samuel became part of the Vallery gang. The police would call her to the station anytime you guys committed a crime. She was asked to give names of everyone who stayed with you and Samuel here. God knows how much trouble was caused to others who lived here. Every time you guys came to the neighbourhood, the whole place was turned upside down by the police looking for evidence,' Joel says and pauses to drink water. John looks on silently. He knew he would have to face this reality sooner or later.

'Because of you two, she had even run out of money,' Joel says.

'But I sent her money regularly,' John says, sounding surprised.

'She despised your money. She didn't have any tenants,' Joel says.

'I tried to convince her to sell the house and move in with us, but she wouldn't sell it. She lived here alone because no tenant would rent the place for being associated with you. She treated you all like her own kids, and because of you and Samuel, she suffered so much,' Joel says. John stands there looking at Joel for a while.

'I wish I could apologise to her personally, but I have to live with the burden. I know that just an apology won't change anything that I did in the past, but all I can do is say sorry. I am sorry,' John sighs. Joel looks away, and John walks out of the house.

He walks around the neighbourhood, and everywhere his gaze wanders, he finds his younger self perpetuating some crime. He feels disgusted with himself so wants to get away from this area. He instinctively boards a streetcar.

'I am sorry, Mrs Russo,' he says, looking back.

'Just the beginning, John, you gotta face more,' he thinks. He knew that this was going to happen.

After a few stops, he gets off and sits on a transit stop bench, reciting the quotation. He feels better after a while and then looks around. He finds himself in front of 'The Swiss Chalet' restaurant. He remembers some of the finest evenings he had spent there.

John was near the Moss Park neighbourhood. He had an apartment in the Moss Park apartment building, but it was auctioned off.

He trudges in the Moss Park neighbourhood aimlessly and finds many tents erected by the homeless in the park. In the corner of the park, he spots some people playing chess. It is late afternoon, and his stomach grumbles due to hunger. He looks out for an empty bench and sits there, savouring the cookies. He looks at the kids, playing in the corner of the park while their parents are either shooting videos, clicking photos, or busy on the phone doing something or talking.

'Looks like they have a severe case of **Sombie Virus*,' he mumbles.

'Play with them and leave the damn thing in your pocket,' he continues mumbling, enjoying the cookies.

He sits in the park thinking about what Joel said, and occasionally he would find tears slipping out of his eyes.

'Don't get all emotional now; you knew this would happen,' he mumbles, wiping his tears.

He takes a sip of water and then looks around. He spots a man sitting alone. The man, it seems, was looking for someone to play chess with him. John walks up to him confidently. He is slowly but steadily losing his prison-style slow walk.

'May I?' John asks, and the man smiles. John sits in front of him.

'I am Solomon,' the man says, extending his hand.

John happily shakes hands with him. 'I am John,' he says.

'You are from around here?' Solomon asks John as they start to play the game of chess.

'Yes, used to, but I had been the government's guest for a long time, so haven't been to the neighbourhood for ages now,' he replies without feeling awkward. Solomon looks at John.

'Same here, man, seven years...but I was young then,' Solomon says. John just nods.

'Fate has brought you to the right man,' Solomon says proudly.

They play for some time. 'Check,' John says, and Solomon looks at his options and smiles. 'Good game, man.'

'You want some more?' John asks, and Solomon smiles. Solomon re-sets the pieces and makes his move.

'Tell me something. Why would everyone rather look at the phones in their hands and not talk to each other? I mean, why can't parents just enjoy the park with their kids and stop looking at their phones?' John asks, looking around. He makes his move even without looking at the table. Solomon quietly looks at his phone kept on the table. He feels awkward and immediately keeps the phone in his pocket.

'Maybe they got more important things happening on their phones?' Solomon says and shrugs; he makes his move. John looks at the pieces and calculates his next move.

'You know even chess can be played on a phone,' Solomon says.

'What? Where's the fun in that?' John asks, sounding surprised.

'Never mind, let's just play,' Solomon says, raising his eyebrows. He makes his move.

'You are right. The world has changed a lot while I was in there; I mean prison cell. Maybe... I need to understand it,' John says, making his move. Solomon loses the game again, and he looks at John with disbelief.

'Were you practising in there?' Solomon says, feeling annoyed.

'You got time for a few more rounds?' Solomon asks, and John just looks back. They play some more rounds, and Solomon loses all. He looks at the watch. It is evening.

'Enough for the day. I am through!' he says, packing his stuff. John keeps sitting. Seeing John not move, Solomon looks back.

'You got a place to stay?' Solomon asks, getting up and holding his cane. John looks at him with a blank face.

'Can you help me with a hotel nearby,' John says, looking around.

'Didn't they provide you the address for a government facility?' Solomon asks.

'Yes, they did, but I don't wanna stay there,' John replied.

'I see, come with me. I got a place where you can crash for now,' Solomon says.

'But you don't know me,' John said.

'Yes, I do, you are John, and I am Solomon, and we both know each other. Now move your behind and come with me,' Solomon says, and John just looks on. John picks up his box, and they walk towards an apartment complex. John is surprised to see the apartment; it is the same apartment complex where John once lived.

John is filled with nostalgia as he looks around. While walking towards Tower-A, they walk past the parking area of Tower C, and John visualises his Beige coloured 1970 Dodge Challenger parked in parking spot number 303. He stands there, looking at the spot for a moment.

'Hey John, you coming?' Solomon says as he sees John looking at the parking space. John quickly catches up with Solomon. Solomon notices John wiping his eyes. 'Wassup?' he asks.

'I lived in this complex once,' John says, looking at the building.

'Really?' Solomon says.

'What a coincidence,' Solomon exclaims.

'Could this be the sign?' John thinks, looking at Solomon.

'Why don't you sit here? I will look around for a while,' John says as Solomon nods.

John walks around Tower-C for a while and comes back where Solomon was waiting for him.

'Nothing much has changed around here except for the parking lot. It looked much better earlier. Cars are quite ugly now,' John says, laughing. Solomon laughs as well.

'Tower-C is for the elite,' Solomon says, seeing John looking at Tower-C.

'I was an elitist once, but an evil one - ruthless and corrupt!' John says, looking disgusted.

'Let's go, nothing else to see around,' John says.

Solomon limps as he walks, and John follows him inside the building. Solomon's wrinkled hands hold the walking stick tightly, in any case. That's the thing about old age. You don't want to let go of the only support you have for yourself. He smiles gracefully as he limps, and his grey hair looks overly neat and perfectly combed.

'How did this happen?' John asks, pointing towards Solomon's leg. Solomon walks towards the lift area and sighs, and the walking stick makes a sound on the concrete floor in the lift lobby.

'You mean this? Oh, a combination of many bad decisions led to a brawl, and I almost lost my leg. Alcohol had a major part in it,' Solomon says shyly while he still smiles at John. They take the lift for the seventh floor, to apartment number 707.

'This is my place; you can crash here,' he says as they enter the modest but elegant apartment.

'Take that room,' Solomon says, pointing towards a room in the east.

John keeps his box on the bed and looks at a child's photograph in the room. Solomon walks in.

'That's my granddaughter, Catian. She's grown up now. My daughter Linda doesn't let me be around her, so this is all I have. I have kept this room for her if she comes over someday,' Solomon says, looking weary. 'Drink?' he asks.

'Sure! I haven't had one in a long time,' John says, winking.

Solomon gets a pizza out of the fridge and heats it in the microwave. They both enjoy the drinks and the pizza. Around 10 PM, Solomon dozes off on his couch. John helps him into the bed and walks down for a walk.

He only walks for a few blocks when someone approaches him, enquiring about an address while showing a piece of paper. Within a few seconds, a car stops behind him, and before he can understand anything, a man gets out of the vehicle and covers John's face with a bag and pushes him inside the car.

They drive for some time and then stop at a place with a pungent stench.

'We must be near the treatment plant,' John thinks after getting out of the van.

Though his face was still covered, he knew Toronto too well. After a while, he finds himself inside a building. He is made to sit on a chair.

‘What is this? Who are you?’ he asks. For someone who had just been kidnapped and driven around, he seemed too calm. A man removes the bag and uncovers John’s face. Another man unties his hands.

‘Sorry about the trouble, John,’ he says and stands in front of John. John looks at the man fluttering his eyes, trying to see clearly. It was a familiar face.

‘Are you little Thomas?’ John asks, looking at the man’s face. The man smiles, and John gets up to hug him. Both laugh and look at each other.

‘Not little anymore. I handle the business now,’ Thomas says confidently and rushes in to hug John again. John hugs back tightly.

‘You look just like your father,’ John exclaims, looking at Thomas. Thomas is William’s eldest son, and now he is the boss.

‘My mother had asked me to take care of you when you come out. But I couldn’t meet as the police have been all around you ever since you got out. I couldn’t get you in trouble, so I had to meet you like this,’ Thomas says.

‘Also, we had to make it look like we ditched you in the prison so that they could go easy on you. So, we kept sending the lawyer to the prison,’ he continued.

‘Do you need anything? I will give you anything for your loyalty,’ Thomas boasts.

‘I am an old man now, and I don’t have many needs. I am going to be alright,’ John says, as Thomas smiles.

‘Anytime you need me, you can call him,’ Thomas says, giving John a card and pointing towards a man John recognises easily. He is the family lawyer who has visited John many times. His name is Hanson.

John thinks for a moment. ‘Can you find Doctor Jim O’Neil for me?’ he says, and Thomas looks back, shaking his head.

‘John…,’ Thomas says, and John jumps in even before he could say anything.

‘I just wanted to give him a courtesy visit,’ John says.

‘You want to give a courtesy visit to the doctor who got you arrested?’ Hanson says.

‘Whatever be the case, he was a good friend, and I just wanted to thank him for getting me arrested,’ John says, and Thomas looks at Hanson. Hanson shakes his head sideways, signalling Thomas against it.

‘You wanna thank him?’ Thomas asks.

‘Ahan,’ John says and looks at Thomas.

Thomas stays silent for a moment and then reluctantly says, ‘He’s in room 325 at Sunrise Senior Living.’

Hanson looked upset. ‘If he wants to find him, he will do it on his own as well. Now that I have told him, get ready,’ Thomas says, looking at Hanson. Hanson just raised his arms and walked away, still shaking his head.

‘What do you mean? Get ready for what?’ John asks.

‘Now that you are out, the cops must be watching the place. One false move, and they will pound on you.’ Thomas sounds concerned.

‘That won’t be necessary. I am just going to say hello. I won’t need Hanson,’ John says calmly. He walks up to Thomas.

‘Thomas, give up all this,’ John says, looking around.

‘Look what happened to your father…’ he continues. Thomas interrupts.

‘We do whatever we need to do to survive, John,’ Thomas says, and John felt as if William was standing in front of him. John smiles.

‘You always wanted to be like your father,’ John says.

‘Leave it all to me. You enjoy your retired life, old man,’ Thomas says, giggling. John looks on calmly.

‘Be careful with Jim.’

'With mom and dad gone, you are the only one left,' Thomas says and hugs John again. 'Good to see you, Johnny.'

They drink together that night, and then after a few hours, John is dropped back at the same place.

John walks back towards Solomon's place when a car stops next to him, and a well-suited guy comes out. He shows his police badge.

'Was that Thomas?' the man asks John.

'Thomas, who?' John lies. The man looks at John suspiciously, pointing his finger at his chest.

'Remember that you are being watched,' he glares at John for a good one minute. After getting no reply from John, he gets back in his car and leaves.

It was already early morning. John quietly walks in and goes to bed. He wakes up after some time, only to find Solomon making breakfast.

'Good morning. Hope the bed wasn't that small for you?' Solomon asks after his greeting.

'No, I slept well,' John says.

'So, what do you wanna do?' Solomon asks as he whisks the eggs in the glass bowl.

'I want to sing,' John replies, and that made Solomon smile.

'You got any blues bars left around here?' John asks casually.

'Plenty, but it's going to be difficult getting an eighty-year-old on the stage,' Solomon laughs out loud.

'I will take you to a Karaoke bar to meet my friend. He knows a few people in the music industry. He will be able to guide us. Let's see how that goes.'

'Thanks, I owe you one,' John says.

‘Don’t mention it. We gotta look after each other,’ Solomon whistles, and John hums a tune.

‘By the way, I am seventy-five and not eighty,’ John says.

‘Not much difference, man,’ Solomon says, giggling as John giggles as well. John helps Solomon chop the tomatoes.

‘If you don’t mind, can I stay here for some more time before I can get my own place?’ John says, feeling awkward, and continues before Solomon could say anything, ‘I will pay you the rent.’

‘Stay here for as long as you wish; in fact, don’t look for a different place at all, just stay here. I could use a little extra money,’ Solomon says, feeling awkward too.

‘No problem with the money. I will pay you rent and buy groceries as well,’ John says.

‘Super,’ Solomon exclaims.

‘I gotta do something important. I will be back in the evening,’ John sighs.

After breakfast, John leaves.

******

John goes to Sunrise Senior Living and enquires about Jim, and surprisingly John is allowed to meet him. He introduced himself as Jim’s old friend.

‘He could use a visitor because he doesn’t have must time left,’ the nurse says as they take the elevator to the third floor.

‘What happened to him?’ John asks.

‘Old age happened to him,’ the nurse replies.

‘Tell me about it,’ John says, giggling, and the nurse giggles with him.

‘There’s a coffee machine in the common area,’ the nurse says, pointing towards the end of the corridor. She knocks on the door and enters room 325.

‘Jim, you have a visitor,’ she says while entering the room.

Jim was sitting in a wheelchair, looking out of the window. He turns around, and John is taken aback. Jim was wearing a respirator connected to a cylinder.

‘I will leave you guys to chat,’ the nurse says and leaves.

‘How are you, old friend?’ John asks. Jim laughs, and so does John.

This wasn’t how Thomas or anyone else would have imagined them catching up after such a long time. They were surprisingly calm seeing each other and considering that Jim called cops while John was unconscious, this was quite peculiar.

‘Let’s go to the common area,’ Jim says as he presses a button on his wheelchair, and he moves towards the door.

‘Are you afraid that I might kill you in here?’ John says, giggling.

‘That would be a blessing, my friend.’

‘Just take my respirator away for a minute.’ Jim says, laughing.

John grabs a cup of coffee for Jim in the common area.

‘I had told the staff in advance that I will have a visitor.’ Jim spoke slowly through the respirator.

‘So, how have you been?’ he asks, taking the respirator off his face. He takes a sip.

‘Fantastic,’ John exclaims, and then there was an awkward silence. They both waited for the other to say something.

As Jim finishes the coffee, he looks at John.

‘You are not here to kill me, then why are you here? Just say it and leave,’ Jim says. He sounds frustrated. John just sits there looking at Jim.

‘Oh, for heaven's sake. Are you here for an apology from me?’ Jim asks impatiently. John doesn’t reply.

Jim continues. 'Fine, if that's the case, then I am sorry that I betrayed...' Jim says, and John stops him.

'I am here to thank you,' John says, and Jim just looks back confused.

'What?' was all Jim was able to utter. He was shocked, just like Thomas and Hanson were.

'Had I not been caught, I would have surely found an excuse to continue what I was doing then,' John says, and Jim looks on silently.

'For too long, I had used bullying and my rage as an excuse to justify my wrong decisions, but the fact is, it was just an excuse. I would have used the same excuse to continue living the same way had you not informed the cops that day.' John looks back, smiling.

'Thank you, Jim,' he says, and Jim tries to soak in what he just heard. This was completely unexpected because Jim had expected anger and rage from John.

'You are a changed man, John,' Jim says smiling. He extends his hand towards John, and John happily reaches out.

'So, what now?' Jim asks.

'You will see. Keep up with the news,' John says and walks away, leaving Jim in a confused state.

John takes a bus to Brampton. He was planning to go to his house, but after the experience with Joel, he was wary of the family's reaction upon seeing him.

He reaches Brampton at around 14:30 PM. It was a trip down memory lane as he walked around. The area had changed a lot in the last fifty years since he left after clipping his hair. However, he is still able to navigate towards # 202 on Abbey Street.

This was the first house his father had bought in Canada. His father had purchased another house in the neighbourhood, but it was here at # 202 that they lived and died. Though his parents were long gone, his uncle's family still lived there.

He looks at the house nervously and tries to gather the courage to walk up to the door and ring the bell. John looks around and then crosses the road towards the house. He finally decides to go and introduce himself.

'Hello, I am John...ahh, I am Jasmeet,' he mumbles as he walks towards the house. The visuals of his parents at his trial flashes through his mind.

*****

The name John Russo became infamous, but his parents always longed for Jasmeet. They would come to the courthouse during all trial dates, waiting to see their son. But their son had long gone, and all they heard was John Russo's name. Firstly, his father died three years after he went to prison, and then his mother too died six years later. Being the only child, John was allowed to cremate his parents. He was allowed escorted visits for the cremation. With each funeral pyre, he felt as if a bit of John was cremated along with his parents and a bit of Jasmeet was restored in him.

After his mother died, he was only left with the guilt and burden; the guilt of disappointing his parents every step of the way in his life, the guilt of abandoning them. John devoted himself to performing various duties assigned to him diligently, and he used music to heal himself. He was able to subside his guilt to some extent by keeping himself busy in prison. Singing also helped him relieve the stress of laborious prison life. He wanted to make good of whatever amount of life he was left with once he got out of prison.

*****

Upon reaching the front yard, he stops near the tree; he looks around feeling nostalgic looking at the Khanda (Sikh religious symbol) on top of the door. The visuals of his childhood at the house crossed his mind, followed by the memories of his father's angry face when he showed up with his hair clipped and afterwards him leaving the house. Joel's voice echoes his mind as well, and suddenly his heart starts pounding, and he feels as if everything around him is spinning.

After he had left home, he had come back many times just to see his mother, but he just couldn't dare to move past the tree and ring the bell, fearing his father's wrath. He would come and stand around the house for hours just to see a glimpse of his mother.

'What if they too are still angry with me just like Joel?' he thinks, and John feels disoriented. He holds on to the tree and breathes heavily.

'I can't face them,' John says.

John notices the door opening and hides behind the tree. A kid comes out to pick up his basketball from the front yard. He sees John standing behind the tree.

'Hey, mister,' the kid says, and John comes out from hiding. The kid looks at John, gives a broad smile, but John quickly moves away from the house and hides again. A lady comes out in the yard, and the boy points towards John's direction, but John moves away from that place and starts to walk in the other direction, just like a zombie would walk. He keeps on his pace and soon reaches Gurdwara Dashmesh Durbar's gate. He instantly walks inside and takes off his shoes, and covers his head.

Then, he washes his hands and feet and goes inside. He sits in the main hall looking at Guru Granth Sahib Ji from a distance. He visualises his mother taking him to the Gurudwara as a child in the same neighbourhood. She used to take part in the Seva (Holy service) as well. He gets up, walks in front of the Guru Granth Sahib Ji, and gets on his knees with his hands joined in respect for the almighty. He bows his head, touching his forehead on the ground. John Sweets Russo vanishes for a moment, and it is Jasmeet, seeking forgiveness.

He stays bowed down for a while until he feels someone is beside him. He watches a toddler who bows down too. He caresses the toddler's head and turns around, and sees that his parents are standing behind him, waiting for him to get up and make way for other devotees to pay respect.

'I am sorry,' John said, getting up. He apologises for keeping them on wait.

He goes back to his place and sits there, listening to Gurbani (holy chants) for some time. Then he goes to the langar hall (eating area), drinks tea, and eats some pakoras. He finds it tastier than any other food he had eaten in the past thirty-four years.

By the time he comes out of the Gurudwara Sahib, it is already afternoon. John gives up the idea to meet his family. After what had happened with Joel, he simply couldn't muster the courage to face his family and instead decides to go back to Downtown Toronto. He looks for the nearest bus stop and takes a bus to Union Station.

*****

It is evening, and John heads towards the park in Moss Park area, where he sees Solomon enjoying a chess game with someone.

John waves at Solomon. Solomon sees John and smiles back.

'BE WITH YOU IN A MINUTE, JOHN,' Solomon says out loud. 'I got this, sucker.' he says, smiling.

'Ha, you bet. I own you,' the man playing with Solomon says with a chuckle.

'Check!' said the man after a few moves, and Solomon looked back, disgusted. John laughs, seeing Solomon lose again.

'Do you ever win?' John asks as Solomon walks towards him.

'Sometimes,' Solomon says, sitting next to John. John looks at him. Seeing John not look away, Solomon feels annoyed.

‘Alright… never. I have never won.’ Solomon giggles and John had a good laugh at his expense.

‘You through with your work?’ Solomon asks.

‘No, not really. I never tried,’ John remembers chickening out and leaving the house without meeting anyone.

‘Well, don’t overthink. It will happen when the time is right,’ Solomon assures. John looks around, dejected.

‘So, don’t mind me asking why you were in prison for so long? What did you do?’ Solomon asks immediately. John looks back silently.

‘You don’t have to share if you are not comfortable,’ Solomon raises his eyebrows in anticipation.

‘My full name is John Russo,’ he says, and Solomon just looks back.

‘Do you know about the Vallery gang?’ John asks, and Solomon observes his face with disbelief.

‘You are John Russo? John Sweets Russo?’ Solomon asks as his voice is filled with excitement and nervousness, all at the same time.

‘Yes,’ John replied calmly.

‘Shit, man,’ Solomon exclaims. He's still not sure if he should be happy or scared.

‘Why do you need to find work? You must be rich,’ Solomon speaks but regrets that very moment.

‘I am in no mood to get back to my previous life,’ John could feel a sense of regret again hovering around him. In an instant, the question transported him back to his past life.

‘I got a lot of money in my accounts from the old days. They still exist, but that was blood money. I don’t want anything to do with it.’ As John says this, a sense of disgust follows his entire being. He regrets immediately and sighs. John gets up and walks around.

‘I did some bad shit back then, and I have nothing to do with that life now,’ he continues.

Solomon mumbles, ‘I could use some money.’

‘What was that?’ John asks.

‘Nothing, man, not your problem. Just that I will be evicted soon. I didn’t pay the bank for some time, and now I am in a huge arrear. Though I am regularly paying now, it's still far from being over,’ Solomon says.

‘I am sorry, man,’ John walks up to him.

‘Hey, not your fault, man. I did some bad things too.’ Solomon quips.

‘I am going to find some work and make sure you don’t lose this apartment. How much time do you have?’ John pats his new friend.

‘Six months,’ Solomon quickly answers. John looks dejected after hearing the timeframe.

‘That’s too little time,’ John made a disappointing face.

‘No worries, we will figure something out,’ John sighs and reassures Solomon.

‘You are a good man. You helped me, gave me a roof over my head without knowing anything about me, and shared food. Now it’s my turn to return the favour,’ John says and pats on Solomon’s shoulder.

‘You are a changed man.’ Solomon says, looking at John.

‘Hope so.’ John smiles.

‘I work at a convenience store nearby. I will speak with the owner for you, and I will call a few people to get your singing career going,’ Solomon’s eyes gleamed as he said that to John.

‘Let’s grab something. I am hungry,’ John says, pointing at a Tim Horton outlet close by.

They return to the park with their coffee and snacks. They enjoy the coffee and snacks and narrate stories from their past. John thinks about Joel and his experience outside his family house in Brampton and decides to take it easy with the walk down memory lane. He chooses to concentrate on his singing first.

**Sombie (Adjective) - a person who is lost in his/her phone endlessly while being oblivious to the world around them - Version One and a Half (version 1 ½).*

KARAOKE FUN

Solomon makes a few calls after coming back to his apartment and speaks about John. Most people refuse to hear about his troubled past and his protracted and rather squalid age, while some were genuinely curious about him and his music and wanted to meet him.

Solomon takes John to a nearby bar the next day.

'Wow! This looks familiar,' John exclaims after entering the Dewberry Street Bar. It is an old-school kind of a place in downtown Toronto, with dark wood interiors and black and white chequered tablecloths. At last, John feels at home because of the positive and friendly vibes. Solomon asks John to sit around one of the tables near the Karaoke setup while he goes towards the office. When he returns, the waiter brings them drinks. Since it is a Karaoke night, the youngsters went on stage one by one to sing their favourite songs.

Few manage to stick to the rhythm while others try to be all over the place, but everyone enjoyed the music. That's what Karaoke is all about; to enjoy the music.

John and Solomon are enjoying the drinks when the manager tells something to the DJ in his ear. The DJ looks surprised, and then he announces, 'We have an exceptional guest tonight. Give a huge round of applause for John Sweets Russo directly from Delimit Institution.' John feels awkward about the DJ mentioning Delimit Institution along with his name. Solomon winks at him.

'Go for it, Sweets, the manager is a good friend of mine, and he has contacts in the music industry,' Solomon pats John. John nervously walks towards the Karaoke stage and looks at everyone in the dining area, enjoying their food and drinks. He is relieved that no one is staring at him even after hearing Delimit Institution, but that is expected from people engrossed in their food and drinks in a bar.

He picks up the mic and looks at the screen in front of him. It is a touchscreen monitor with a list of songs and a search bar.

'How do I?' he says, fiddling with the touch screen.

Seeing him struggle, a young man walks up to him. 'Here, let me help you, grandpa,' he says, smiling as John gets out of the way. John whispers in his ear, and he searches for the song. The young boy giggles at John's choice.

'This should be good,' the boy says sarcastically, walking back to his table. He whispers in the girl's ear sitting at his table, and they both giggle. John is still smiling, though. He isn't bothered about the giggling.

The music starts, and Solomon whistles and shouts, 'GO FOR IT, SWEETS!'

John starts to sing "My Way" by Frank Sinatra with confidence. As he sings, the visuals of his mother run through his mind, and his eyes become moist. He sings like a professional singer, and everyone stops eating and drinking and just listens to John's voice. John soon closes his eyes to feel the lyrics. He remembers every single word of the song. He opens his eyes only when the music stops. Everyone in the bar claps for John and starts shouting, 'More, more, more…' as John steps down.

'Ladies and gentlemen, Mr John Sweets Russo,' the DJ announces, and Solomon rushes towards John and pushes his newfound friend back onto the Karaoke stage.

John sings "Eight days a week" by Beatles, and the place comes alive, yet once again. Solomon passes John a drink. He takes a sip and looks at four Sikh men sitting across a table next to the stage.

'If you permit me another song, I want to sing something exceptional,' John asks shyly, and to his surprise, everyone in the bar cheers for him. Seeing the crowd's reaction, John signals towards that table and one of the Sikh young man walks up to him. John says something, and he looks back as if he has seen a ghost.

'Really?' he asks. John does not look like an Indian, so when he asks him to search for a Hindi song, the young man is surprised.

'What's your name?' John asks.

'Paramjeet,' the boy replies while looking at John. John admires his pagri (turban).

'Play it,' John says.

'Okay, let me search for the song.' Paramjeet says and searches for a Karaoke track on the touchscreen monitor. He plays the song and then stands next to the stage.

It was music for "Mei Jatt Yamla Pagla Deewana (Mad, crazy, mad)," an old Hindi song. John sings the song joyfully, and the South Asian's in the bar are amazed to hear John sing a Hindi song. This song gets all of them dancing and grooving. The others, who did not understand the lyrics, still move to the peppy music. John perfectly syncs the lyrics with the music being played. His Hindi and Punjabi accents are still up to the mark.

John ends the song on a high note with a Punjabi call, 'HADIPPA (HURRAY).'

Everyone in the bar was ecstatic and eager to shake hands with John as he stepped off the Karaoke stage. John walks back towards Solomon.

'What was that?' Solomon asks excitedly as John sits in front of him.

'I didn't know you could speak Indian,' Solomon asks, and John shrugs.

'India is a country, my friend and the countrymen are called Indians, but there is no language called Indian,' John says, smiling. He gulps an entire glass of water.

'Really, then what language do Indians speak?' Solomon raises his eyebrows.

'There are many languages in India, like Hindi, Punjabi, Bengali, Tamil, etc. This song was a mix of Hindi and Punjabi,' John says.

'Fascinating! But how does an Italian know so much about India and that accent, man? That was wow! You sang like them!' Solomon asks after he takes another sip of his whiskey.

'My parents were Indian, and my real name is Jasmeet, John is the name I chose to feel like a Canadian, and Russo is the name I chose when I moved out of my house,' John says, looking overly dejected.

'I gave up everything dear to my parents just to feel like a Canadian,' John says, keeping his head down. His hands play with the whiskey glass, and he watches the drink. Solomon looks back silently.

'...and the sad part is that no matter how much I try, that part is long gone, I can't get it back,' he says, referring to his parents, who are no more. Solomon looks at John silently. The sombre mood on their table is broken as Paramjeet arrives at their table, along with his friends.

'Bro, that was awesome,' Paramjeet 's friend said joyfully.

'Glad you liked it,' John replies, shaking hands with all of them.

'Their bill is on us,' Paramjeet calls the bartender.

'Wow, that's great. Let's get something packed now that they are paying,' Solomon laughs at his own joke. He was teasing the boys.

'No need, boys,' John says. Solomon gives him a look for refusing the freebies.

'Thank you, guys. I am highly obliged, but we are all right,' John continues. The boys go back to their table.

'You need to get used to the free stuff, my friend. I see you becoming famous very soon,' Solomon giggled as he savoured a piece of chicken.

A man comes to their table.

'Hey John, meet Sam. Sam, this is John,' Solomon introduces them ecstatically. 'Sam's the guy I talked about,' he whispers while winking towards John.

'How do you do, sir?' John says, extending his hand towards Sam. Sam shakes hands with John and joins their table.

'You, sir, have an extraordinary voice. I am impressed,' Sam says.

'Thank you!' John replies, smiling.

'Saying that…' Sam says and pauses. John and Solomon look at him in anticipation. '… there is the thing about your past,' Sam feels awkward as he said that.

'I checked about you and found a lot of stuff online. The people I work with might have a problem…' he says, and John gets up and leaves before Sam finishes.

Solomon comes out after a while and sees John standing outside, waiting for the streetcar.

'I am sorry,' John says as he sees Solomon walk up to him. The streetcar stops in front of them, and they both get on board.

'No, I should apologise for what Sam said,' Solomon says as John looks out, disappointed.

'I don't know why I reacted this way because I knew this would happen,' John says. 'I can't run away from my past,' he clenched his fist in anger.

'Hey, don't you worry, man, I will get you connected for sure.' Solomon pats John.

John smiles but deep down, he knows it is going to be tough.

*****

The next morning

'Hey, hey, hey…' Solomon rushes in, all excited. He shows a flyer to John. It was an announcement for Canadian Talent's (CT) Toronto auditions for Season 10. John curiously looks at the flyer.

'It is a talent show where people sing in front of an audience. You must go there.' Solomon says ecstatically.

'You don't need people like Sam telling you that you can't do it. Contestants from all backgrounds can perform here, so you better get going,' Solomon winks at John.

'I need to listen to the latest songs,' John insisted. Solomon passes his phone to John.

'One-stop shop for everything, my man!' Solomon gushed.

'Teach me how to use it and help me get one as well, so that I don't keep borrowing yours.' John maintains, and Solomon teaches him how to use a smartphone.

John works at the convenience store along with Solomon. The auditions are only a few days away. In the meantime, Solomon and John go to Karaoke bars, and John performs, enthralling people everywhere. Although it was pretty tricky working at the convenience store during the day and singing at night, he was determined to practise for the talent show.

John buys a smartphone, and he would listen to the latest songs on YouTube and practise them.

*****

John is busy scanning the items through the barcode machine at the counter when he notices a girl staring at him. She stands at the counter, waiting for John to tell her the billed amount while staring at him. He finds it weird and continues with his work, but the staring continues. John finally looks up, and she looks away awkwardly. He again gets busy with scanning the items, and the stare continues.

'Do you… need a bag?' John asks awkwardly.

'YES…' she replies.

'That will be $74.28,' John smiles and observes that the girl's gaze is still hooked on to him. He immediately stops smiling.

'Credit, visa,' she says while still looking at John. There was an awkward silence as they both looked at each other.

She taps the card on the card machine, and John passes her the receipt. She quickly collects the items in a bag and leaves in a hurry. The girl stops at the door and turns around to look at John. She then fiddles with her phone and rushes back towards John. John sees her coming back and feels strange vibes but smiles, nonetheless.

'Did you forget something, miss?' John says to the girl who looks at her phone and then at John.

'I KNEW IT; IT'S YOU!' The girl exclaims.

Solomon had been noticing this from a distance. He walks up to the counter. 'John, let me handle the counter; you go ahead.' He takes over the counter.

John walks towards the girl and looks at her phone. It was a video of him singing while Clyde played the piano at the Union Station. Someone had recorded the video and posted it on Youtube.

'I love your voice, sir,' she says and looks at John. John looks at her, perplexed.

'I am Kavita, Kavita Kabira,' the girl introduced herself.

'Ah… I am John,' he says.

'How can I help you?' John asks politely.

'I first heard you sing at the Dewberry Street Bar. You remember the boy who helped you play?' When she said that, John went into thinking mode.

'I was there with him. I just loved your voice, and then I saw the video. So when I saw you at the counter, I wanted to meet you,' Kavita says excitedly.

'Nice to meet you, Miss Kabira,' John bows down to the girl.

‘My real name is Kavita Bhutani,’ she reveals.

‘Pleased to meet you, Miss Bhutani.’ John smiles at her.

‘I am a poet, and I was wondering if you could lend your voice to one of my songs?’ She makes a puppy face. John just stands there looking at her as if the cat got his tongue. Seeing John stand there silently, Solomon immediately jumps in. He was listening to the whole conversation.

‘He is going to the CT auditions, and he would be delighted to use your song!’ Solomon exclaimed. John was speechless.

‘Thank you so much for this, and I don’t know what to say. I am speechless by your generosity.’ John replies humbly to the girl.

‘It is I who should thank you for accepting my song,’ Kavita says, folding her hands.

Over the next few days, Kavita shares many songs with John and John selects a beautiful song called ‘There’s a place far away.'

John manages to find a piano at a school in the neighbourhood. They allow him to play the piano in the evening. He practises the song by Kavita rigorously.

THE SHOW

John quickly clears the first round of the show with his rendition of “Concrete heart” by Great Lakes Swimmers. His performance was well-received, and he was handed over an invitation for the next round. He was saving Kavita’s original song for the next round.

June 08, 2014

Two weeks after the first round, John and Solomon reach Ed Mirvish Theatre early for the next round. John marks his presence at the reception desk and notifies that he needs a piano for his performance. A colossal queue is seen outside the theatre. John and Solomon stand in the line for three hours and then in the waiting area inside, for another two hours before John’s turn finally arrives.

John is sitting around and looking at other contestants. Some of them are nervous, while others practise their acts. Solomon looks at John and pats him on his shoulder. He sits next to John and asks, ‘Nervous?’

John looks him in his eyes and says, ‘Solomon, I was only nervous when I picked up a gun for the first time, but never after that have I ever been nervous in my entire life.’

‘Confused, maybe, but not nervous,’ John chuckles and then laughs at himself, thinking about what he has gone through ever since he came out of prison.

‘You are a bad man.’ Solomon says, looking at the nervous contestants. Solomon knew how John felt.

John sees Kavita walk towards them. He gave a polite and charming smile to her.

‘You think I was going to miss this?’ Kavita smiles, and John hugs her.

‘Thank you so much for this.’ John says.

‘All the best. I will be cheering for you in the audience,’ Kavita says and leaves.

‘John, you are up next. Line-up!’ A crew member came and alerted John. John and Solomon stand near the stage entrance, watching a group perform. After the performance, all four red crosses illuminate with the buzzer sound. All four judges reject the group, and John and Solomon watch them walk back with their heads down. They leave the room disappointed.

‘Pretty tough,’ Solomon says, looking at the judges.

‘Ya, that happens when you have been sitting and judging for the past five hours. It's been tough today,’ Patrick, the host, says.

‘How are you today, sir?’ Patrick asks John.

‘I am doing fabulous.’ John replies with a smile. The crew members quickly set a piano on the stage for John’s performance. Patrick gets the cue from a crew member.

‘You are on. GO.’ Patrick directs John towards the stage.

The Judges look up at his face as the audience cheers for him. John stands on the X mark on the stage, admiring the crowd, and then gives a quick look at the Judges; Peter, Latifa, Jamie, and Paul.

‘Welcome,’ Judge Latifa says first.

‘Thank you, it’s an honour to be here, in front of such a huge crowd and this prestigious stage,’ John tries to become comfortable with the surroundings.

‘What's your name, and how old are you, sir?’ Judge Paul asked John.

‘My name is Joh...’ he says and then pauses for a nano moment.

‘My name is Jasmeet John Russo, and I am seventy-five years young,’ John replies and smiles at the judges.

The Judges chuckle together as John introduces himself as young.

‘That’s a unique name,’ Paul comments.

‘And, what do you do for a living or what did you do for a living,’ Paul asks. This one statement makes John anxious for a few seconds. He looks at Solomon standing in the corner along with the announcer.

‘Go, John,’ Solomon whispers, cheering him up. John smiles, looking at the audience, and says, ‘I was a guest at the Delimit Institution for thirty-four years. I enjoyed my stay there, but you know, thirty-four years, sheesh… you do get bored, so I left the place.’ As John reveals this, the whole arena went quiet.

The judges watch him, dumbstruck. They look at each other and then at John. Each one of them felt numb after John’s revelation. After a brief gap, Latifa breaks the ice, ‘What a colourful life you had!’

‘O... too many colours,’ John replies, smiling. He notices something as his gaze turns towards the audience who were whispering. Some audience members check his identity on their mobile phones and constantly talk to each other and point fingers at him. Presumably, they are searching for John Russo online and have found everything about him available in the public domain.

‘That’s Johnny Sweets,’ someone whispers, looking at an article. Even the Judges are alerted about John through their earpieces by the crew.

‘What will you do for us today, sir?’ Latifa finally asks John. There was awkwardness in her voice.

‘I am going to sing an original by Kavita Kabira, who is here somewhere...’ John looks around the hall and clears his throat. Kavita cheers for him, and the audience too surprisingly cheer for him. Kavita’s voice is lost in the vast audience.

It was overwhelming for a person who just came out of prison and tried to set his foot in a new life with new people. John becomes emotional but never nervous. He is still standing and smiling at the audience. His eyes damp, but they know how to live his life now.

'Wow, an original!' Paul exclaims as the audience cheer even louder. Latifa looks around, seeing the overwhelming response from the crowd.

'Alrighty, sir, the stage is all yours,' Latifa says joyfully, pointing at the entire stage floor. John sits on the stool in front of the piano and adjusts the mic.

'Should we take him off the stage?' There is a whispering going on backstage amongst the crew members.

'No, let it be,' someone commands on the radio backstage, and Solomon smiles as he folds his arms around his chest to listen to his friend.

John takes out a paper from his pocket with notes for the song and places it in front of him. John checks the piano and looks towards his left side at Solomon, and gives a thumbs-up. Solomon smiles, seeing John's confidence.

John closes his eyes for a moment and visualises his mother encouraging him to play the piano.

He plays the tune on the piano and gets in sync with the music quietly as everyone waits for him to sing. Some audience members look at each other, assuming that John has forgotten the lyrics, and the whispering voices can be heard across the hall.

He soon gets into the rhythm and starts singing…

'There's a place far away

It was supposed to be my home

I had the power to guide the meteorites

I could enlarge my being to overshadow you

I could kill the way God does

And control the darkest fears in you

Then when I lost my way to paradise

The stars mocked in my eyes

As I lost the place

I thought was home

Behind the destiny's bars, I sat alone

Tears of fire I shed while earth quivered

My stomach cramped with pain as it slowly simmered

In the darkest of my night

I heard a cuckoo sing a phrase so right

She took me to the world of music

A language I didn't know was an epic

So why do I sing to the souls of the dead

Changing constantly

Playing a game of gloom...'

Only his voice is audible in the hall, along with the piano notes, and no one even blinks. There is complete silence as he sings. The judges are actually mesmerised by his voice quality. The waitlisted contestants are also looking at John in awe as he sings and appears on the screens in the waiting area. The waiting contestants stopped whatever they were doing to look at who is singing. Some are moving along with the music and humming the song.

John continues.

'Hey! Where are the dreamers

The lovers, the protectors

Where are my men quietly singing a song

Tell you, I sing for you,

I sing for your soul

Come join me now take control

Let the ugly subside

Bring on the deeper vide

Love I more worthy with a glass of wine

Soft breath, cool breeze

Every cell of the darkroom give it my music

See the new you is born...'

John sings with his eyes closed and only opens his eyes when he is through with the entire song. He looks around; there is a sabbatical calm inside the hall- a profound silence, as everyone is still in a trance after listening to his soulful voice.

John smiles since he is sure he has done a great job. He looks around, hoping that maybe his mother is also sitting there seeing him perform. But he knows that this is wishful thinking, and so he just smiles.

'Thank you, Kavita!' he says and stands there, holding on to the mic tightly.

Kavita looks around, and there is pin-drop silence in the hall. Everyone looks at the stage in disbelief. She stands up and whistles, and the sound of the whistle echoes throughout the hall. Solomon claps with joy, and suddenly everyone gets on their feet with thunderous applause for John. Three of the judges, too, stand up in admiration and clap.

John stands there amidst the deafening applause in the hall.

The clapping and cheering continue for a few minutes when one of the judges turns around and signals the audience to sit down. As everyone gets back to their seats, only Kavita is left standing and cheering. John is happy to see her.

'That is Kavita,' John says, pointing towards her, and she immediately ducks, feeling awkward.

'Wow, that was just wow, John! You are wow! You are amazing, and thank you, Kavita, for writing this amazing piece!' Latifa exclaims as the audience whistle and cheer.

Latifa looks back, searching for Kavita, who was still trying to hide in her seat. A few people around her encourage her to stand. She stands up awkwardly, waving firstly at John and the judges and then at the audience around her. She immediately sits back, taking a sigh of relief. She was not ready for the limelight but was happy for John.

'Thank you!' John replies shyly, looking around. He blushes as judge Latifa complements him. He is still holding the mic tightly in both his hands.

'See that? This means you are good!' Latifa exclaims, pointing towards the audience. John throws a flying kiss towards the audience.

'John Sweets, everyone!' she announces as the audience repeat their claps and cheers.

Meanwhile, John's performance from the first round is played on the massive screen behind the stage, and the cheers get louder. John could hear his voice, but he had no idea that the video played in the background.

'You are right, sir! You are seventy-five years young. Your voice is amazing, and you have the energy of a twenty-something!' Judge Peter exclaims. He is still looking for words to praise John, but he stands up and claps for him again. He then points at the screen, and John turns around and is surprised to see himself on the screen.

'Thank you, sir. Thank you.' John turns around and bows down at the audience and the judges.

'You love Toronto, don't you?' Peter refers to John's choice of song for the first round.

'You bet, can't imagine living anywhere else in the world. Toronto rocks!' John raises his fist in the air, and the audience follows this with loud cheers, 'TORONTO, TORONTO….'

'Toronto truly rocks! I can only say that I am honoured to have been a witness to this amazing performance. It is an emotional song, and your voice has the depth and the variation needed for this song. Bravo!' Judge Jamie complements John with all her heart.

'Thank you,' John replies, and he looks at the fourth judge, Paul, who just sits there, unimpressed.

‘This has been a long day, and I thought it would only get worse when I saw you walk in...’ Paul said.

‘… and then your introduction added to the pain, and I thought, what can an ex-con sing? But…’ he said, making a whacky oddball face.

People at the back booed as they are unimpressed by Paul’s comments. He pauses and turns around, staring at the audience.

‘But?’ John speaks on the mic, and Paul turns his attention back towards John.

‘But…but then you started singing, and the world stopped, and all I could hear was Johnny Sweets. It was as if you were the Pied Piper, and we were the children following you. It was, just like Latifa said, WOOOOOW!’ Paul exclaims as he stands up, clapping continuously.

‘Johnny Sweets, Johnny Sweets…’ everyone screams at the pitch of their voice, and the screaming and clapping rocks the entire hall.

‘Thank you!’ John cries out. The audience’s reception humbles him. It all appeared hallucinatory to him for a single moment.

‘Let me be honest with you, John, you have had a past life, and you have been in prison for enough years, so what is it that you are trying to achieve by coming to this show?’ Peter shoots this question as soon as the audience calms down a bit.

‘I am looking for a second chance in life…’ he says and then pauses for a moment.

‘Well, actually, let me rephrase that. I am looking to make a come-back, and I know my age is not on my side, so I gotta move fast. You know,’ he said, smiling, and everyone laughed.

‘All right then, let’s vote.’ Peter looks at the other judges, and they nod.

‘It’s a huge yes from my side.’ Latifa raises her hand.

'An even bigger Y.E.S. from me,' Jamie says, teasing Latifa.

'A YES from my side too!' Peter says, and then he looks at Paul.

'Guess what? I will save your time by sending you straight to the live shows!' Paul gets up and pushes the golden buzzer in the centre of the judge's table. The whole stage is covered in confetti, and the golden show lights illuminate the entire stage area.

The audience jump in joy as John moves straight to the live show round of the competition, thanks to the golden buzzer.

It is hard for John to understand what just happened. He has no idea what a golden buzzer means. Solomon rushes in, and John looks at him, totally confused.

'They have given you the ticket to move to an advanced round,' Solomon explains while hugging John.

'You are there, man! You are there!' Solomon says, with tears in his eyes. Paul rushes to the floor and places his hand on John's shoulder. John turns around and sees Paul standing there with his hand stretched out. John walks up and shakes hands with Paul. The audience cheers him even louder.

'You have a gift, and you really did well.' Paul says with a thumbs-up amongst the thundering applause of the audience.

He walks back to his seat. 'He's amazing,' he says, taking his seat and looking at other Judges.

'I love this job.' Judge Latifa says, turning around as the crowd still celebrates the golden buzzer.

Solomon and John walk off the stage. John waves towards the Judges and the crowd as he walks out. Patrick, the host, gets hold of John as he reaches backstage.

'JOHNNY SWEETS, how are you feeling?' Patrick asks joyfully.

'On top of the world!' John replies ecstatically. John and Solomon walk towards the waiting area, where everyone gets on their feet, clapping and cheering for John. John becomes emotional, seeing such a response.

'I wish mom would have been here to see this,' he mumbles as Solomon hears him.

'She's there, man; she's clapping for you from up there.' Solomon says and hugs John again.

'Let's go, home man, I am tired,' John says.

John collects an envelope with a timetable and instructions for the next round before they leave for home.

It is already late when they reach home. John cooks a tasty Mushroom-Sausage Ragù and Lasagne for dinner celebrating his success in the contest. Solomon and a couple of his friends from the neighbourhood enjoy the meal with wine. They all chat throughout the night.

'I had once worked for the Vallery gang,' Eugene says, sipping wine.

'Oh, you did? Who was your point-man?' John asks. John was never uncomfortable talking about his past if anyone else started the conversation but never took the initiative to discuss it himself.

''Franky Two Timer' was the point-man,' Eugene replies in a straight tone. 'I used to move liquor for him in my truck, those days,' he says.

'Aaah yes, Franky,' John says, remembering the old days.

'He was handling the Park area.' Eugene says.

'So, why did you leave?' John asks curiously. Solomon listens closely as he knew this conversation was about to blow up.

'I met the woman of my dreams, and her only condition to marry me was if I gave up working for the gang. So, I moved away from here and returned only when I heard that Franky was killed,' he looks at John and says.

'I had heard that you had pulled a hit on Franky,' Eugene says, and Solomon quickly gets up, covering his mouth.

'I do remember Franky and why we called him Franky Two Timer. He died in an accident,' John says as Eugene nods in agreement.

'Did I say it was a hit? No, he had an accident. You are right. It's the memory you know and also the alcohol,' Eugene says, laughing awkwardly pointing towards his head. John laughs out loud, as does everyone, and they all party through the night.

*****

After fifteen days

'Hey John, wake up,' Solomon says, rolling up the blind curtains. John covers his eyes with the blanket.

'It's my off today,' John says, and Solomon giggles.

'You are all over the place, man,' he says, looking at the newspaper.

There's an article about John's performance. John quickly gets up and looks at the paper.

'John, the Hitman Singer, rocks CT stage with a scintillating performance followed by a golden buzzer,' he reads the article.

'You are a celebrity now, man,' Solomon said ecstatically, zooming through the room as if he was doing the waltz as John looked on smiling. John gets off the bed and joins Solomon in the waltz.

'Get freshened up quickly. Today we are going to find you a date,' Solomon winks. He goes out and comes back with a jacket.

'Wear this, man. It would help if you looked good,' Solomon passes the jacket to John.

BINGO

They arrive at the Bingo Hall on Dufferin Street. 'So, this is where I will find a date?' John smiles as Solomon buys Bingo tickets.

'Yup, this is the place,' Solomon exclaims.

Solomon waves at two ladies and walks towards their table.

John stops immediately after seeing the ladies. He feels awkward and is glued at one place.

Solomon looks back and finds John standing afar. He walks up to John and holds his hand.

'Come, let me introduce you to them,' he says, pulling John towards the table. John reluctantly walks behind Solomon.

'Hello, ladies!' Solomon exclaims. They don't even react, but Solomon takes a seat opposite them. They look like they are in their '60s.

'John, here you go, sit,' Solomon says, pulling a chair for John. The ladies look at Solomon silently.

'This is Cindy, and this is Sylvia, John- ladies!' Solomon says as he introduces everyone.

'You can leave Cindy out; she's with me.' Solomon whispers, and Cindy throws the cap of a soft drink bottle towards Solomon. Solomon moves aside, and the bottle cap zooms past John.

'With you? Hah!' Cindy says sarcastically, sipping from the straw in the bottle.

'She's just angry with me. Why don't you say hello to Sylvia over there while I try to pacify Cindy,' Solomon says and moves his chair next to Cindy. John looks at him angrily.

John thinks that his friend is acting funny and weird. He looks at Sylvia nervously, who is busy arranging Bingo slips in front of her. For the first time, he is in the company of a female; well, almost in the company.

‘Today, I feel lucky; I am sure I will win today,’ Sylvia declares.

‘Do you think I will be lucky today?’ she asks, batting her eyelashes at John.

‘I suppose yes. I feel it’s a lucky day,’ John replies awkwardly.

The announcer starts calling numbers on the mic, and Sylvia gets busy listening carefully and keeps all Bingo slips in front of her. She highlights the numbers being called excitedly.

‘Son of a b****,’ she makes a face in frustration as someone nearby stands up and calls out ‘Bingo.’ Sylvia looks frustrated. The announcer again calls the numbers, and Sylvia gets more frustrated as she doesn’t complete any of the tickets.

‘Do you wanna take a walk?’ Sylvia asks as John looks at Solomon and Cindy chit-chatting.

‘Don’t worry, he ain't gonna miss you when he’s with her.’ She says as they walk out of the hall.

They stroll around. John chats with Sylvia while looking around.

‘Solomon tells me that you are from around here?’ Sylvia asks, and John looks at her.

‘Yes,’ he replies, looking around.

‘So, why did you leave?’ She asks.

‘I was ordered to leave,’ John replies with a smile.

‘You were involved in any crime or something?’ She shoots the question, but John simply smiles.

‘You don’t follow the news much, do you?’ John clears his throat as he says that.

‘What are you, famous or something? Anyone hanging out with Solomon can’t be famous or rich,’ she finally lets out a chuckle.

'I am known as John Sweets Russo,' he reveals and then looks at Sylvia, who looks back at his face as if finding some answers.

'I am sorry, I thought Solomon had already told you,' John gulps. Sylvia looks back at John closely.

The curve on her cheeks finally returns. 'You look quite young on the television!' Sylvia exclaims and then suddenly blushes as she recognises John.

'I should've known it was you,' she says, still smiling and looking at John from top to bottom. 'Can't blame you; I do look different on the tube.' John shrugs and smiles.

'HEY JOHNNY MAN, you left me alone in there,' Solomon screams from a distance, and Cindy punches him. He is walking towards John. John looks back.

'I mean, you left us alone in there,' Solomon says, smiling. Cindy gives him an angry look.

As Solomon gets closer, he notices a gun popping out of the window of a car coming from the other side.

'JOHN!' Solomon screams and rushes towards John. Before John could react, Solomon tries to pull John out of the way, but the bullet hits Solomon in the abdomen. The car vanishes in a nanosecond, and John holds Solomon tightly and tries hard not to let him fall on the sidewalk.

'CALL 911!' Sylvia screams to a young man standing with the phone to his ear. He was in shock and kept staring at all the blood.

'CALL 911,' Sylvia screams again, and the young man quickly snaps back. He immediately disconnects the call and calls 911, and an ambulance arrives, taking Solomon to a nearby hospital. Solomon is moved into surgery as soon as the ambulance reaches the hospital.

While Sylvia and Cindy are waiting in the reception area with bated breath as Solomon is operated on, John walks around angrily. He uses the hospital's payphone to call Hanson and narrates the entire incident with a message,

‘Tell Thomas that you guys need not touch them. I will handle it. Just find out who did it, and I will owe him my life.’

‘Don’t do anything stupid. Let us handle this,’ Hanson says. John disconnects the call and comes back. Cindy was in tears.

‘He’s a tough son of a gun; he’s gonna make it through.’ John assures Cindy and signals for Sylvia to come aside.

‘Is this because of you?’ Sylvia asks.

‘I don’t know. I don’t know who would do this to me?’ John sighs. John looks at his jacket; it was covered in blood. He quickly takes it off and places it on a chair.

‘I need to talk to you!’ a man stands next to them and says to John. John can see his detective badge displayed on his belt. He takes John aside.

‘We have already given our statements to the police,’ John says. He is looking distraught.

‘I understand what you are going through. But I am not here to take your statement,’ the man says, and John looks on curiously.

‘Now is the time to open your mouth and spill the beans about the gang. They have tried to kill your friend, and you are still trying to protect them even after more than thirty years,’ the man continues, and John listens quietly.

‘I didn’t catch your name?’ John asks.

‘I am Detective Sanchez, and I am with the organised crime division,’ Sanchez replies, showing his badge.

‘Detective Sanchez, I have no idea who did this. I was convicted of the crimes which I had committed, and I completed my sentence. So, I don’t know what information you are talking about?’ John replies with a shrug.

Detective Sanchez is taken aback by John’s attitude; a man who was sad due to his friend getting shot some moments ago and the man with a new mindset now. After observing the expression on John's face for a couple of seconds, Sanchez walks away.

The doctor comes out of the ICU after a while.

'The bullet didn't cause much damage, but the shock and blood loss combined with his age and high BP might cause some complications. We will know for sure by morning,' the doctor says, and John just walks away silently, leaving Sylvia and Cindy with the doctor. It feels to him as if he cannot hear anything, and his vision is getting blurred. He is about to fall when Sylvia comes and holds on to him and helps him sit on a waiting chair.

'This can't be real.' he mumbles.

'I need to get out of here. Stay with Cindy, and don't worry about the money!' he stands up as Sylvia looks at him, confused.

'You can talk to me.' She keeps her hand on John's shoulder as a sign of assurance.

'Don't do anything stupid. You got out clean,' Sylvia says, and John is thankful for having such good people around him. He looks back admiringly.

John smiles. 'I am going to be alright,' he says as Sylvia looks back, concerned.

'Don't worry, I just need some air. I will be back soon,' he says and walks towards the exit.

As he steps out of the hospital, he is mobbed by the media with multiple cameras being pointed at him and the reporters speaking together with the mic in their hands only inches away from John's mouth. John is not in his senses. He is sweating, and all he hears are muffled voices around him.

'John, has your friend been shot because of you?' John can finally comprehend one of the reporter's questions as he gets back to his senses. John looks at the camera. He just walks away from everyone, even as the reporters keep shouting. He has no idea where he is supposed to go and just keeps walking.

After some time, he comes back to his senses and calls Hanson, the lawyer, from a payphone. John quickly briefs Hanson.

'Let us handle it, John. You take care of your friend,' Hanson says and disconnects the call.

John was in no mood to relax; he takes out a small diary from his pocket and dials a number on the keypad.

'This is Autumn,' was the greeting as the call was answered.

'Hello Autumn, this is John Russo,' John said.

'It's an honour, my cousin from the prison told me about you. How can I help you?' Autumn says.

John quickly tells Autumn.

'Where can I reach you?' Autumn asks, and John tells him his phone number.

John gets a location on Whatsapp after about fifteen minutes with a message, 'Be here by 10:00 PM.'

John takes a taxi and reaches the place well in advance. He walks around and scopes the site from all directions; it was a warehouse in Vaughan. As John enters the main gate, he is stopped by security.

'My name is John Russo, and I am here to see Autumn,' John says while looking at a CCTV camera. The security guy receives instructions on his radio, and John is taken into a massive building. The place was full of people moving boxes on conveyor belts and loading them on trucks.

John is taken into a room that was filled with people wearing security jackets. They were roughing up two men tied up on chairs. Their mouths were gagged with duct tape.

'It was easy to find them,' a man said as John looked at the two men being beaten black and blue. The man signals, and his men back off.

'I am Autumn,' the man says, getting up. He shakes hands with John. 'It's an honour to meet you in person, Sweets.'

The word 'Sweets' sends shivers down their spine, and both men look at each other.

'Who are they?' John asks, looking at the two men angrily.

'This one's Oscar, and he is Kasim. They are low life thugs for hire, and they usually hang around this area,' Autumn says and pulls the tape off their mouth.

'Why did you shoot at me?' John asks as their faces wore a blank flabbergasted expression.

'Are you the John Sweets Russo?' Oscar asks. John just looks back. It was hard to decipher if John was angry just by looking at his face.

'We are sorry. We didn't want to shoot you,' Kasim says, shaking with fear.

Both men just whimper, looking at John.

'We just wanted to scare the other guy by shooting him in the leg. He wasn't answering our calls,' Kasim said, sobbing.

John thinks. 'The other guy? You mean Solomon?' John says, but Kasim remains silent, and so does Oscar.

John walks closer to them.

'WHO DO YOU WORK FOR?' John screams, picking up a long nail from a nearby table. He also picks up a hammer and rushes towards the two men. The two men plead and beg for mercy as John places the nail on Kasim's knee.

'They would kill our families if we told you their names. We just collect money, man,' Oscar says, sobbing.

'THAT'S ENOUGH!' a man said, walking towards them. It was Hanson whom John had called earlier.

'Why didn't you wait?' Hanson says as he takes the hammer from John's hand.

'You don't need to get involved in all this,' he says, looking at John, and then he looks at Autumn angrily. Autumn looks away, feeling awkward.

'He works for us,' Hanson says as he looks at Autumn.

'How did you find me?' John asks.

'You think Thomas will leave you unprotected. We are always watching your back. Now go,' Hanson says as John looks at the two men.

'Let us handle it. You need to stay clean,' he says, pleading for John to leave.

'Drop him near the hospital,' Hanson says as Autumn nods.

A car drives John back to the city.

'Just drop me here,' John says. They were still a few blocks away from the hospital. John gets out of the car and walks towards the hospital.

He must have walked for a few blocks when a taxi stopped next to John, 'Get in, you will get tired walking,' the driver says, and John gets into the taxi.

The taxi waits at a traffic light, and the driver carefully looks in the rear-view mirror. He then picks up even as the light is red and drives straight. Many vehicles come to a halt as he jumps the traffic light. John looks back and sees a black car stuck in between the intersection. It was the same detective's car he had met after meeting Thomas for the first time.

The taxi drops John near an Art Gallery opposite St. Claire station.

'He's waiting for you,' the drivers said before leaving. John enters the Gallery and sees Thomas standing in front of a painting and admiring it.

'What do you think?' Thomas asks, looking at the painting as John stands next to him.

'Seems like the mother is protecting her baby,' John says.

'Really, where is the baby?' Thomas raises his eyebrows.

'It's not yet born,' John replies, and Thomas again looks at the painting carefully.

'Oh ya, you see, that's what I call an art lover.' Thomas says, looking at his bodyguard standing at a distance. The bodyguard looks back with a stoned expression on his face.

'Aah, never mind,' Thomas says and looks at John.

'Who do they work for? Was it the Charlie gang?' John asks impatiently.

'No, it's not them. When Piero, Charlie's son, heard about this, he called me personally and assured me that he wasn't responsible for this. We've been at peace for twenty years.'

'Past is past, and I buried my anger a long-time ago. We have our areas earmarked. So, I wouldn't worry about Piero,' he says, assuring. Thomas sighs, looking at the painting.

John is surprised as he knew that it was hard for Thomas to bury the past, considering Piero's father Charlie had his father killed.

'You are more matured and smarter than your father,' John says, taking a seat. Thomas looks at John teary-eyed.

'I have learnt to handle my anger, as should you,' Thomas says, dragging a chair opposite John.

'I will tell you who they work for, but you have to promise me to not pull the kind of stunt you just pulled ever again,' Thomas says and looks at John. John looks back silently.

'Listen, you got out clean, and very few of us get that chance. So, you gotta make sure that you stay clean. Alright?' Thomas says and waits for John to reply.

Sylvia's voice echo's through John's head, telling him the same thing.

'Please…' Thomas says, making a babyface.

'Okay, I promise,' John says, smiling.

‘Thank you!’ Thomas exclaims.

‘What do you know about Solomon?’ Thomas asks as John looks back silently.

‘What do I need to know about him?’ John asks.

‘He was in prison for many years!’ Thomas raises his voice.

‘I know that.’ John says impatiently.

‘He was arrested for smuggling narcotics and went to prison for seven years,’ Thomas says as John just looks back. He already knew this.

‘Do you also know that he is addicted to gambling and fell into bad debt; because of this reason, the casino guys nearly killed his daughter? He still owes them money,’ Thomas says as John looks back, shocked. Solomon had never shared this.

‘The goons said that they had targeted Solomon to make a statement. They work for a casino owner, and it had nothing to do with you. They shot at you by mistake because you were wearing Solomon’s jacket. But as it happens, Solomon came between you and the bullet and got shot,’ Thomas reveals as John sits silently listening to Thomas.

‘I can handle the casino guy. He will not harm Solomon ever again. Piero handles the Niagara area. But you gotta make sure he never gambles again.’ Thomas says, and John just nods in agreement.

‘By the way, you look good on TV. We loved you on the stage the other day. Papa loved your singing, and so did momma!’ Thomas exclaims, shaking hands with John.

Thomas drives John to the hospital and stops the car away from the front gate of the hospital. They both get out of the car and walk towards the hospital.

‘Thank you.’ John sighs. Thomas looks at John, lost in his thoughts.

'Is Sanchez bothering you?' Thomas asks, and it breaks John's reverie. He is surprised at the question as he didn't mention Sanchez during his conversation with Thomas.

'We got your back, man! You know that.' Thomas says, holding John's hand. John smiles. Thomas then walks back towards his car, leaving John at the hospital's main gate. Thomas makes a call as he drives away.

John sneaks back inside the hospital without being spotted by the media and finds Cindy and Sylvia in the waiting area. Sanchez was sitting close by.

John stands at a distance. Sylvia walks up to him.

'How's he?' John asks.

'He's awake but still not out of danger,' Sylvia says with a faint smile.

'He's awake? At least some progress,' John wipes the sweat on his forehead.

'How's she holding on?' he asks, looking at Cindy.

'Don't worry about her. She knows that Solomon has had a troubled past, so she doesn't blame you for this,' she replies.

'Did you know that Solomon had a gambling debt?' John asks Sylvia.

'No! Even Cindy doesn't know about the debt. He had promised her that he would quit gambling,' Sylvia replies with her eyebrows shot up.

Sanchez walks past them, smiling.

'Isn't that the detective who was bothering you earlier?' Sylvia asks. John simply winks and then looks at Sanchez.

'Have a good one, Sweets.' Sanchez says as he walks away.

Thomas did say that he will take care of everything, and it looks like he did. John thinks about Thomas and the conversation they had.

'Never mind him, he will not bother again,' John tells Sylvia.

'Can we see Solomon?' John asks.

'Not until tomorrow morning,' Sylvia replies.

'Okay, there's nothing much we can do here. Let's all go home and come back tomorrow morning. You guys need to rest.' John says.

'As do you, John,' Sylvia says, and John nods his head.

John and Sylvia firstly drop Cindy, and then they go to Solomon's flat, where they continued chatting. John makes coffee, and they sit on the balcony.

'How did an idiot like Solomon meet a caring lady like Cindy?' John asks and giggles. Sylvia laughs.

'He might be a compulsive gambler, but he's a nice human being. Cindy was in a lot of trouble, and he helped her and stood beside her. They've had an on and off relationship ever since, but they love each other,' Sylvia says, taking a sip.

'Yes, Solomon's a nice guy,' John sighs.

*****

Next morning

John, Sylvia, and Cindy reach the hospital.

'Let me check with them,' Sylvia walks towards the nurse station to check. The senior nurse allows them to visit Solomon.

John carefully opens the door, ensuring his friend doesn't get disturbed. He stands near the bed as he remembers the stage, the judges, and the claps. He was thinking of Solomon, who was right next to the stage, cheering and clapping for him.

Solomon wakes up and sees John standing there looking at him. He tries to remove the respirator covering his mouth. John rushes in and stops him from taking it off. Solomon is trying to say something, and every time he speaks, the respirator is covered with frost. John can barely hear him.

'Don't speak; you need rest,' John tells Solomon and holds his friend's hand. Solomon still tries to speak, so John removes the respirator temporarily.

'I am sorry, sorry man...,' these words come out of Solomon's mouth finally, though he is still finding it hard to breathe. John instantly gets the respirator back on his face.

'It's all right, buddy. I know about it,' John caresses his hand.

'Promise me you will never gamble again.' John says as Solomon nods his head, holding John's hand.

The next day he gets a visit from a man from the Talent Show's team. John is informed that his name has been removed from the list of contestants because of whatever happened.

'The show can't be dragged into any kind of controversy, especially when a contestant is involved in a shooting incident. Since the investigation is still going on, we can't take any chances. Hope you understand and will refrain from making any statements about this in public,' the man says calmly. John would have explained everything, but he just didn't feel like explaining himself. He silently walks away.

GOING VIRAL

John, Cindy, and Sylvia visit Solomon every day. It takes about a week for Solomon to recover. His problem with the casino guy is resolved, thanks to Thomas.

Solomon is in for a pleasant surprise as he reaches home.

'WELCOME…' there is a loud cheer as Solomon enters the house; arm around John's shoulder, he limps.

'Welcome back,' John smiles as he holds Solomon tightly.

'Thanks, man!' Solomon exclaims and then hugs John. Everyone gathers around Solomon while John helps Solomon sit on the recliner. Solomon looks at the recliner; it looks brand new.

'This is your welcome gift,' John says as Solomon admires the recliner.

'Thank you, everyone. This means a lot,' Solomon says with watery eyes. Cindy and Sylvia cheer for Solomon as well. John passes a glass of scotch to Solomon. 'To your health,' John says, taking a sip. Solomon takes a sip feeling grateful to John.

John soon gets a call and goes to the other room to speak. Solomon looks on as John returns.

'Here's your main welcome gift,' John says as a girl enters, followed by Solomon's daughter.

Solomon looks at the girl with disbelief and then looks at John, who stands there smiling.

'Thank you!' Solomon exclaims. It is his granddaughter Catian along with his daughter Linda. Solomon becomes emotional looking at Catian and Linda together. 'This is the best day of my life!' Solomon exclaims and cries out. These are tears of happiness and joy.

'Thank you, John; you are an angel. Your mother was right,' Solomon says, and that makes John emotional too!

Solomon calls everyone, and they gather around him.

‘This celebration is not just for my return but also for John winning the CT trophy very soon. To the superstar!’ he says, raising a toast. Everyone looked around awkwardly.

‘What's wrong?’ Solomon asks, and John looks at Cindy and Sylvia.

‘They cancelled my gig,’ John reveals.

‘Is that because of me? Tell me the truth. Damn!’ Solomon starts to curse himself.

‘I can’t do anything right. This was your second chance, man, and I screwed it as well. Just like I have screwed up my own life,’ Solomon continues while sobbing.

‘It wasn’t you, man; my life was screwed long before I met you,’ John interrupts him.

‘I will find another way to sing,’ John says with an assuring smile.

Solomon sits there quietly, feeling dejected. John tries to cheer him up, but Solomon feels guilty.

As the night falls, it is just Solomon, Cindy, Sylvia, John, and Pauline, Sylvia’s grand-niece present, sitting and chatting about things.

‘Pauline and I were talking about this while coming here. Listen to her,’ Sylvia says as John comes back to the room after helping Solomon to bed. ‘The man was quite tired.’ John says as he takes a seat on the comfy couch next to Pauline.

‘John, you have an amazing voice, and Uncle Solomon said you could also sing in Indian and Italian,’ Pauline says as John looks around, hearing about ‘Indian’ again.

‘No one is going to give me a chance because of my past,’ John says, feeling disappointed.

‘We will not go to anyone, but we will make sure people come to you,’ Pauline says with a positive tone of voice.

‘We will create a YouTube channel for you and post your videos singing in English, Indian and Italian,’ Pauline announces as everyone looks at her.

‘It is Hindi!’ John says.

‘Say what?’ Pauline asks.

‘Never mind. You were talking about a YouTube channel? What is that?’ John manoeuvres the question.

‘Yes, I have a band, and I know a social media guy who will set up everything. We don’t need anyone’s permission to create content for the web. Let people decide if you are good or not.’ Pauline says.

‘You think people will listen to an old man on Youtube?’ John sighs as he watches Pauline cringe.

‘You bet!’ Pauline says.

John smiles, and Pauline and Sylvia look at each other ecstatically.

Pauline helps him create a YouTube channel, and a young guy named Lionel helps John set up his social media accounts.

His channel is aptly named ‘The Gangsta Grooves by Jasmeet John Sweets Russo’.

Recording takes place at Pauline’s house. She has a small recording studio in her basement with essential equipment. She would also edit and process the final videos here. Everyone waits for John in the recording studio on the first day. The band members rehearse as Solomon, Sylvia, and Pauline wait for John.

‘I hope he won’t be a no-show because of nervousness?’ Pauline asks, and Solomon giggles at her anxiety.

‘Girl, you have no idea about John, do you?’ Solomon laughs sarcastically, and finally, they hear someone walk down the basement stairs. John walks down, and everyone looks at him, surprised. He enters the basement wearing a

Pagri (Turban) and smartly dressed in black Punjabi Kurta Pyjama.

'This is the real me, and far too long I have pretended to be someone else. Now it's time for the real me to come out,' John says proudly. Solomon and Sylvia smile while Pauline looks on silently.

'Do you think people of other ethnicities will connect with your look?' Pauline raises her eyebrows in disbelief.

'This is not a look; this is who I am!' John says with a straight face.

'This is going to work, trust me!' Sylvia adds in her trust and confidence in John, while Solomon nods in agreement.

'Did you handle the copyright issue for the songs I shared?' John asks.

'Why hurry for the copyright? Let's just post the video and see the response first,' Pauline says.

'Take it from me; planning is the key for staying out of trouble. If you are right about this and the video indeed goes viral, then the first thing everyone is going to check is the copyright,' John says and looks at everyone.

'I am just kidding, grandpa,' Pauline says. 'It's all in place,' she says, smiling.

John wears the headset and takes his place in front of the piano. He closes his eyes for a while. He recites the verses given by his mother before opening his eyes and facing the camera. They want to shoot the videos in an unplugged format. They have already rehearsed the song for the inaugural episode.

'Sat Shri Akal (Sikh greeting), hello, I am Jasmeet, and I am a Sikh by birth, but everyone knows me as John Sweets Russo, a name and identity I chose fifty years ago. You see, I felt that if I gave up my heritage and accepted what I thought was Canadian, then those who made fun of my looks would probably accept me. But, I was actually trying to run away from who I was. I have lived this pretentious life far too long, and today, with this video, I am returning to my roots.'

'Remember that no matter how much your bullies push you around and harass you, crime is never the answer. It was like a negative spiral, and I kept making bad choices.'

'I got what I deserved for my bad choices, and this is me making a comeback.'

'I believe that whether I look like and sound like an Indian or an Italian or a British or French or a Greek or a Pakistani or an Iraqi, I would still be a Canadian at heart because Canada is what it is because of people from these rich cultures making Canada their home. Canada is what it is because of all of us and not one community, and no matter what anybody says, don't ever give up on your heritage. Be a good Canadian but also remember your roots. Here's presenting Gangsta Grooves…' he says and raises his hand with a thumbs up.

Pauline sees the sign and starts the instrumental music. It was instrumental music for "Ajj Din Chadiya Tere Rang Warga" by Rahat Fateh Ali Khan.

John hums to the music just like a professional singer would do and also plays the piano. John observes that Sylvia and others cannot understand the lyrics due to the language barrier. Still, he is elated to see how his friends are enjoying the music and Sylvia and Solomon are tapping their feet on the floor, and Cindy is snapping with her fingers. She seems to enjoy it as well. John feels proud of himself and his friends.

As John finishes the song, he looks at the band members, and they give the intro to "You Don't mess around with Jim" by Jim Croce.

Pauline and others are amazed by John's energy. This is a high-energy, fast-paced song, and as John sings, it feels as if John is a twenty-something and not seventy-five-year-old.

‘This is for my wonderful Italian friends. Pardon me if my accent is off, as I only know basic Italian,’ he says before starting the next song.

He sings “Bella Ciao (Goodbye beautiful)”. Though he sings only a few phrases, he is still able to create an impact. Everyone enjoys the session.

As John stops singing, the band members get together, praising John.

‘This was for Samuel and St. Jamestown,’ John says as he remembers Samuel and Mrs Russo.

Pauline gets on the mic and says, ‘Let the revolution begin, Bella Ciao.’

‘Thank you, guys,’ John says, showing his appreciation for the band, Pauline, and Sylvia. Pauline and Sylvia get up, sending thumbs up from the control booth.

*****

‘That’s wild!’ John exclaims, looking at the first cut of the video on Pauline’s laptop. Lionel posts the video on multiple social media platforms.

The first video is received with a mixed response, with many people praising John for going back to his roots while others criticizing him for his past.

John personally looks at all the comments on Pauline’s laptop and smiles.

‘You knew this was going to happen,’ he mumbles, going through the comments and reactions.

His second video with his rendition of “Singing in the Rain” by Gene Kelly is received quite well, and the negative comments go down quite a bit. The video garners ten thousand views within four days of being posted online with hashtags such as #gangstagrooves #talent #desigrooves #everyonedeservesasecondchance #secondchance #redemption going viral in no time.

Lionel regularly promotes the videos and also creates a website for better reach. Soon the videos became popular across many platforms. But they were still far from what they had wanted to achieve.

Twenty eight videos and almost four months down the line, they meet at Solomon's place for discussion. It was December 23, John's birthday, and they had gathered to celebrate the day but ended up forgetting the birthday because of the serious discussion.

Many people still didn't want to be associated with John, and the team was concerned about the revenue. Though they were making some money, that was not enough.

'Slow and steady wins the race. Have patience, guys.' John says, seeing the younger lot rack their brains to generate ideas. Paulin, Lionel, and the band members they all discussed as John craved for their attention. Sylvia and Solomon just look on, making some kind of snacks in the kitchen.

'I wanted to sing, and we are getting a lot of views. Why are you all worried?' John shrugs.

'We have to figure out how to make more money. Otherwise, Solomon loses his house, and I will lose my studio.' Pauline says, and they all get back to their discussion. John is taken aback, and suddenly he remembers Solomon's bank loan.

'Last time I tried to make quick money, I became a criminal,' John mumbles, looking distraught. His voice was lost in the chaotic discussion. He waits for his chance to speak.

'What we need is shock and awe to go viral. We need some tie-ups and sponsorships,' Pauline says. John walks around and looks at Solomon. Solomon nods.

'I have an offer to perform at a place,' John says as all eyes finally turn towards him.

'You have an offer?' Pauline asks admiringly.

'Well, why didn't you say so earlier?' she says as everyone rush towards John.

'Tell us, tell us….' everyone exclaims together, and John feels as if he is being hounded by reporters. Sylvia rushes in, 'Give him some space.'

John breathes easily and then laughs unexpectedly.

'Too much excitement,' John says and grabs a chair.

'Sit please,' John says calmly.

'Come on then,' Pauline says impatiently while sitting.

'Solomon,' John looks at Solomon.

'Children lend me your ears,' Solomon sings, and there were smiles all around.

'Now, we oldies may not know about this social media thingy, but we do understand that shock and awe sell,' Solomon gushed.

'That's what we are trying to figure out, grandpa,' Lionel quips.

'We got something for you but, before we can share the news, can we celebrate John's birthday first?' Solomon announces, and Sylvia gets the cake with a seventy-six shaped number candle.

'What, no space for seventy-six candles?' Lionel says and giggles.

John cuts the cake, and Sylvia brings in the prepared snacks and a bottle of wine.

'So, what is it?' Pauline asks impatiently while munching the cake, and Solomon looks at John. John gives a mysterious smile.

'Well, we got a shock and awe for you,' Solomon says as Pauline and others look back in anticipation.

'John has been invited by the jailer of the Delimit Institution to perform on their inception day. It's an extraordinary occasion, and a lot of dignitaries will be there,' Solomon says, and the younger lot just look back with their jaws dropped.

'Look… we know that prison…' Solomon says, and Pauline jumps the gun without letting him complete his sentence.

'THAT IS AWESOME!' she exclaims, looking at Lionel, who looks ecstatic as well.

'It is!' Solomon announces as he already prepared a script to convince them and not expected them to agree with him even before he finishes his sentence.

'Yes, this is it. This is going to get us a lot of publicity!' Pauline exclaims.

Solomon and John look at each other. They feel overwhelmed.

Sylvia brings in sandwiches for everyone.

'Don't worry about the crew for the video. I got a nice group in my college. They will do it for free,' Lionel adds in.

'It's set then; we are doing this,' Pauline shows a thumbs-up. John is upbeat about performing in the same prison he had served for so long.

This gig was going to be unique not only because it was the first one for John but also because they had planned to include some prisoners.

The prison compound was converted into an arena for the show.

John and the band, along with members from the prison, practised round the clock over the next few days. Simon with acoustic guitar, Kevin and Douglas with bass guitar and Don, Kelly, and Laura were added to the group for background vocals and harmonies. They were prisoners and were practising along with John and the band for the show. Laura also had a few solos lined up. Meanwhile, Lionel was promoting the event on social media platforms.

'Guys, I just met Kalm and guess what? Someone saw our online promos for the concert and has decided to join us!' Pauline says ecstatically and pauses. John and others from the stage look at her in anticipation.

Pauline and Sara, the event coordinator, had just met Kalm, the jailer, to discuss a few things, and he had informed them about this development.

Pauline continues, 'The ex-Chief Justice saw our promo, and she has found this to be a great platform.'

'She is a good friend of the outgoing Commissioner of the Correctional Service of Canada. The ex-CJ wants to use this platform to honour the outgoing Commissioner,' Pauline continues and looks at others on stage and around her. Everyone just stands there dumbstruck, staring at her.

Pauline looks at everyone. 'Ah… guys?' Pauline says, and like a Mexican wave, everyone raises their arms in the air with joy and cheer at the pitch of their voice. It was as if their favourite player had just scored a goal.

Loud Joe, who had been assigned to work with John and the crew for the show, hugs John. Joe knows how much this concert means to John; he feels delighted.

John smiles, looking at Pauline, and then he looks up at the sky. This was the chance he had been looking for. Loud Joe holds his hand up as if John had just won a boxing match. Things just got bigger with the ex-CJ and the Commissioner of Correctional Services being there.

Lionel adds to the icing on the cake when he informs John that the social media is abuzz with the hashtag gangstarocksjail trending all over. The entire concert was to be broadcasted live on Youtube. While John didn't understand the technicalities of social media, he was thankful for the hard work Lionel and his team were putting in.

'Hey John, you remember Sam?' Solomon asks John, who was standing next to him.

‘Yes, your guy from the karaoke bar,’ John replies.

‘Well, now he seems to be interested in you,’ Solomon says with a wicked grin.

‘I leave it to you, man,’ John laughs, and Solomon immediately disconnects the call. John smiles.

On D-day, the stage was set for a grand concert. Over twelve hundred people were in the audience, including who’s who of the law enforcement and corrections department from across Canada. Families of the Delimit Institution prisoners were also present, along with the prisoners seated in a separate section. With just a modest ticket fee, the Youtube live video was viewed by over 200,000 people online.

John enthralled the audience with many classic tracks while his fingers moved effortlessly on the piano. He was supported by little Clyde on the piano. He was specially invited by John for the event, and his mother gladly let him be a part of the concert. She cheered for him from the crowd.

Laura’s soulful rendition of "I am a woman" by Helen Reddy and "A Natural Woman" by Aretha Franklin captivated everyone.

The Highlight of the evening was John’s rendition of an original song on the piano. Just John singing and playing the piano on the stage, and the audience was mesmerized by his voice.

Loud Joe and other cellmates were quite excited about John performing this song. John had been humming this song for over twenty years, and this was the first time he had performed it in front of an audience, so he was very excited. Pranay was John’s cellmate briefly, and he had written this especially for John.

'I have come too far, I have come too far, I wanna get back to from where it all starts...

There was a line people fear to cross, a destiny they can't dare to choose... But I somehow managed to climb up the hills; yes, I chased my dreams...

I miss the smell of that Lilly flower, I miss my mom's gift of that li'l car...'

As he sings, the visuals of his mother go through his mind. He gets emotional but manages to control the rhythm.

'I have come too far, I have come too far & now I wanna get back to where it all starts...

To get what's there to earn, I forgot all that took years to learn...

Happiness, sorrows, big & small, trust me, darling, I have seen them all...

Behind all I got, there is nothing beneath

I miss my mom, my dad every time I breathe.

It's up to you to make it cry of war or sound like a sweet jingle of a guitar...

I have come too far, I have come too far, now I wanna get back to where it all starts...

God has given me more bye's than Hies, but that hope still flies high above the skies...

Instead of the bad returns, I always chose the right doings; it's one of the things that keeps me moving...

Of that big sky, I feel like a broken star...

I have come too far, I have come too far, now I wanna get back to where it all starts...

I made mistakes & wrong turns, Ignored the bests, I chose the silly ones.

I tried many things in life but can't properly sit; what to say now I have done my bit...

Hope is the only thing that can take you far...

Yes, I have come too far, I have come too far... now I wanna get back to where it all starts...

I have come too far, I have come too far...'

'This was penned right here in this institution. May God bless Pranay, wherever he is,' John says, and there's a massive cheer from the prisoner's section. John waves at the area.

John raises his arms in the air in the middle of thundering applause from the crowd. With moist eyes, he calls on everyone to come on stage. Pauline, Solomon, Sylvia, and Lionel, along with the band members, join John on stage. He and everyone else in the team takes a bow to the audience.

'Thank you for all the love and adoration. Everyone deserves a second chance,' he says and looks at the section where all the prisoners were seated. They all cheer for Sweets.

'You have given me my second chance. I love you all,' he turns emotional when he says that. He passes on the mic to the MC.

In the following days, the video garnered more than five million views and was trending everywhere. Part of the money earned from the concert was donated to the Correctional Board of Canada. Pauline was able to rent a better place, and she created a studio with state-of-the-art equipment.

Now, everyone wanted to work with 'Gangsta Grooves by Jasmeet John Sweets Russo'.

John and the band continue making videos. Their format involving multiple languages in each episode was quite unique, and the channel became a hit not just in Canada but across many countries.

He also collaborates with Kavita & other songwriters and composers for originals in English, Hindi, and Punjabi, along with recreating hit songs.

John and the group are invited to many prominent shows and news channels. Everybody wants to know the story of the real Jasmeet John Sweets Russo.

He starts receiving massive fan mail and messages through the post, email, YouTube, Instagram, and other social media channels.

In the mails and messages, he sees many messages from a person named Simerjeet, who mentions that he is the son of Harminder, John's uncle. But John could never gather the courage to reply. Every time he wanted to respond to Simerjeet, he would remember Joel's angry face.

Over the next few months, they get multiple sponsorship deals and shows. They were now touring across the world, and the brand Jasmeet John Sweets Russo got even more prominent.

In Nov 2016, John incorporated a music company, The Heritage Recording Company, giving ex-cons and new singers and artists particular preference. At the company's launch party, John bumps into Latifa, the 'CT' judge. She is a famous singer herself.

'Sat Shri Akal (Sikh greeting),' Latifa says as John smiles.

'Sat Shri Akal,' John responds, bowing his head in respect.

'It was the show's loss,' she says and then pauses for a moment. She is clearly referring to John being axed from the show.

'Life moves on. No matter how much you try, life will not stop. You gotta keep moving,' John says, and Latifa smiles in agreement.

John's first album, 'Jasmeet John Sweets Russo', was a smash hit and topped charts across Canada, the USA, and Europe. It was a combination of English, Italian, Hindi, and Punjabi songs. Something never tried before.

Their tour bus with 'Gangsta Grooves by Jasmeet John Sweets Russo' painted all over it receives massive reception wherever they travel for a show. They travelled through the length and breadth of Canada, doing shows round the clock. It seemed that age had no impact on John's energy; he gained more and more fans with each live performance and video.

Solomon pays off his loan with the bank, and he too makes good of the second chance he got thanks to John.

THE SECOND CHANCE

Solomon and Cindy get married at a beautiful ceremony at Palais Royale's deck on Lake Shore Boulevard, overlooking Lake Ontario, in the fall of 2018. John is the best man and is elegantly dressed in a Pagri and black suit.

A photoshoot takes place with the groomsmen and bridesmaids after the wedding ceremony at the lakeshore. Though the average age of groomsmen and bridesmaids was about seventy years, their enthusiasm is no less than any teenager present at the party.

At night, Sylvia and John take a walk across the Sunnyside Boardwalk and enjoy the nighttime view of Toronto city across the lake. The moonlight reflecting on the surface of Lake Ontario is breathtaking. They sit on a bench near the lake and enjoy the sound of waves hitting the lakeshore.

They look at the deck area of Palais Royale, which is lit up with party lights. The music is audible even where they are sitting, and they can see people grooving to the music.

Sylvia wanted to talk about John's past, and John answered all her questions without hesitation. John wanted to be honest with Sylvia, so he narrates many grim details. Sylvia could sense the discomfort on his face as John recounted about his misdeeds.

'Let's talk about something else…' Sylvia says, seeing John uncomfortable.

'Did you know any celebrities back then?' she chuckles, trying to change the mood.

John happily narrates the night he met Claudio. John's boss had close contacts with many celebrities. Sylvia was amazed to hear about John meeting so many stars.

They sat there enjoying each others company when John notices a shadow at a distance. It was dark, and John couldn't clearly see who it was. The man walks towards them, and his face is apparent as soon as he steps in the limelight of a lamp post. It was Thomas.

‘Stay here.’ John walks towards Thomas.

‘Can I steal John for a moment?’ the man says, waving towards Sylvia. Sylvia looks concerned but smiles, nonetheless.

‘Be right back,’ John says as he sees a worried look on Sylvia’s face.

‘Sorry,’ Thomas says again, waving towards Sylvia.

Thomas and John walk behind the treeline in the park.

‘They are keeping a close watch on you and Solomon,’ Thomas says as John looks on.

‘They want to know if my money is involved in all this. They could also be tracking your old accounts,’ he continues while pointing towards Palais Royale.

‘I haven’t touched those accounts. I don’t want that money.’

‘There is nothing to be found because every penny is accounted for,’ John says confidently.

‘Hope Solomon is clean now?’ Thomas asks.

‘Yes, he is,’ John replies.

‘Okay, I will keep you posted. Here, this is for the happy couple,’ Thomas says, passing a paper bag to John. There’s a gift-wrapped box in the bag.

‘I wanted to give it to him personally, but…’ Thomas says and pauses.

‘Say no more,’ John says, and they walk back to where Sylvia was sitting.

‘Everything alright?’ Sylvia asks, seeing John and Thomas.

‘Couldn’t be better,’ Thomas says, smiling. ‘Pleasure to meet you,’ he exclaims as John sits beside Sylvia.

‘Thank you for looking after him,’ she says, holding John’s hand. Thomas smiles and leaves.

Sylvia and John look at each other, and John is about to say something when he hears an announcement on the mic, and they laugh. They listen to the announcement carefully; Solomon is screaming on the mic, ‘HEY SWEETS WHERE ART THOU?’

‘Looks like Solomon is missing you already,’ Sylvia says, and John stands up, extending his hand towards her. Sylvia happily holds his hand, and they walk back towards Palais Royale. Sylvia looks at John while walking. John firstly doesn’t notice her glare as he kept walking, looking at Palais. He suddenly sees her eyes hooked on him.

‘What?’ John asks jokingly as they walk hand in hand. Sylvia stops and punches him in the stomach. ‘Ouch!’ John says, holding his stomach and giggling.

‘You dumb a***.’ Sylvia snarls.

‘We are alone, and all you can think of uttering is just one word. You can sing in front of millions but can’t say the magic words to me?’ Sylvia was furious, and she leaves John’s hand and marches towards the party with a thumping sound.

John rushes after her and holds her hand. He pulls her closer and gently kisses her. Sylvia keeps her eyes closed as she stands closer to John. She opens her eyes only to find John looking at her, holding her hand. The time freezes as they stand there for a while.

Solomon gets on the mic again and constantly calls John. John giggles and takes a step back. Sylvia looks around awkwardly and then hugs John. They both walk back towards the deck. Solomon is drunk as hell and jumps towards John as soon as he walks in.

‘Ladies and gentlemen, I present to you, The Incredible Mr Sweets,’ Solomon announces and pulls John towards the stage. Sylvia sits in front along with Cindy. Sylvia places the paper bag on the table.

John sings “Lady in red” by Chris De Burgh, and Solomon and Cindy dance on the floor slowly. All eyes were on them as they slowly moved to the music, and after a while, other couples joined them on the floor. John follows this with his rendition of “Can’t take my eyes off you” by Frankie Valli. Sylvia sits there blushing. His rendition of “Stand by Me” by Ben E. King was the icing on the cake. “Wonderful Tonight” by Eric Clapton was like a magical incantation that made the couples lost in each other's eyes. John completely sweeps Sylvia off her feet with "Ain't no sunshine when she's gone" by Bill Withers. Everyone was having a ball on the dance floor as John sang non-stop.

John and Sylvia also join them as the band takes over from John. The celebrations continue until the following day.

HOMEWARD

'Are you sure?' Hansom is shocked.

'Yes, damn sure,' John says.

'Alrighty, it's your money. It will be done,' Hanson says.

After an anonymous tip, Sanchez was able to zero down on five accounts at different banks under fictitious names and money in the tune of eleven million dollars was seized. Accounts could never be linked to John or Thomas.

'WOW,' Solomon exclaims, seeing the amount mentioned in a newspaper article. John and Sylvia smile as Solomon reads from the article.

John's financial transactions were closely monitored by the law enforcement agencies, but there was nothing wrong. John made an honest living in his second chance. After some time, all investigations were closed.

Sylvia calls John. 'I need you to come down,' Sylvia says as John answers her call. 'All right, I am coming down,' John replies.

John had moved into a different apartment in the same building. John comes down the apartment building and spots Sylvia waiting on the other side of the road in her car.

'Where to?' John asks after getting inside the car.

'You will see,' she just smiles.

They drive for a while, and John is taken aback as he recognises the place. She was moving towards Brampton.

'You would not dare,' John warns, sounding angry as he notices that she is driving towards the same house. Sylvia keeps driving.

'I can't do it,' John says as she stops the car in front of house # 202.

'Yes, you can! You know why?'

'Why?' John looks puzzled.

'Because I have been talking to them,' Sylvia says, holding his hand. John looks back angrily.

'John, you can face a huge crowd while singing and not even blink, but you can't reply to your own family?' Sylvia says.

'What were you thinking, John? They got in touch with you, and you didn't reply?' Sylvia retorted, and John's expressions changed from being angry to apologetic in a second.

'You weren't going to reply, so I did,' Sylvia said and got out of the car.

'Now quit being a cry baby and get your behind out of the car,' she said.

Seeing Sylvia not relent, John reluctantly gets out of the car and stands there, looking at the house.

'John, you wanted to sing after you got out, and you are doing that beautifully. But they deserve to see you as well,' Sylvia says and holds his hand tightly.

'It's going to be alright. I promise,' she says, looking at John. John smiles. She rings the doorbell.

'I am here with you,' Sylvia says, seeing John feeling nervous.

The door opens, and a man is standing there. John's reluctance now changes to an overwhelming love when he sees the man smiling.

'I am Simerjeet,' the man says and hugs John. John hugs him tightly. Simerjeet is John's cousin, who had contacted him earlier. He looks almost as old as John.

Sylvia and John walk inside the house. John looks around and sees his father and mother's picture on the wall. He gets emotional, looking at the photos.

'I am sorry,' he says as Sylvia holds him.

'They would be proud of what you have achieved, John,' Sylvia says, looking around.

'Do you still play?' Simerjeet says, and John looks towards him in disbelief. Simerjeet was standing next to the same piano that his mother had bought him. John admires the piano teary-eyed.

‘She bought me this piano after fighting with dad,’ John says, looking at Sylvia. John goes around touching the piano like a kid who had just found his toy.

‘I can’t believe that you guys kept it,’ John says, playing. He closed his eyes and could visualise his mother enjoying it while he played as a kid.

‘Nothing has changed, John,’ an elderly Sikh gentleman coming down the stairs says, and John immediately stops playing and gets up. He feels shameful and lowers his head. The man walks towards John and places his hand on John's shoulder. It is his uncle, Harminder, his father’s younger brother. He is ninety-eight now.

‘Harinder, Jasmeet is finally home,’ he says with moist eyes looking at the photo of John’s father.

‘I was scared of coming back because he was angry with me when I left the house. He wouldn’t like me coming back to this house,’ John says, looking at his father’s photo apologetically.

‘Angry with you? He missed you till his last breath,’ he says, as John touched his feet (Mark of respect in Indian culture). As John gets up, his uncle hugs him tightly. They both cry a bit while hugging each other.

‘Harinder never hated you. He was angry with you for sure, but that subsided after a few days, and he always knew that you would come back. He never said this openly, but he missed you big time,’ uncle’s voice choked as he said that.

‘All he wanted was to see you one last time, but he could never make it out of the house after you went to prison,’ he continues. John’s whole being is suddenly engulfed with guilt and sorrow. His uncle holds his shoulders and looks at him proudly.

‘They would be proud of your achievement today. Never feel guilty again. You have made your parents and us proud,’ he says, and John finally gave a faint smile.

‘This is your mother’s journal,’ Uncle hands over a brown cover diary to John. John holds the journal with shaken hands and looks at it admiringly. He feels scared to open it.

‘So, these are my grand nieces and nephews?' John asks, looking at everyone in the room. Simerjeet has two sons, who were married as well, and they all lived in the same neighbourhood along with their kids. So many generations of the family were there. Sylvia is amazed to see such a huge family.

Joint families are on the verge of extinction, even in India.

John is happy to see everyone together, and all his fears about the family not accepting him vanish in a single moment.

‘Everyone introduce yourself, please,’ John says as he and Sylvia sit on the couch. The kids line up, introducing themselves, one by one.

John and Sylvia also enjoy Indian snacks. Sylvia loves the Samosas, though she thinks the chutney to be a bit too spicy. She savours other Indian dishes as well.

In the evening, John leaves the place satisfied that he could finally come back to his parents and roots.

‘You gotta do something else for me,’ John says as they leave Brampton. He tells Sylvia an address, and she enters the address in the GPS. It was Joel’s address in St James Town.

John sits in the car looking at the street leading to Mrs Russo’s house for a while and then gets out of the car.

‘I gotta do this alone,’ he says as Sylvia waits in the car.

John rings the bell, and Joel opens the door and sees John standing outside. John walks to the house where he lived and looks at the house. He sits on the stairs, and Joel comes and sits next to him. They both sit there silently for some time.

‘You know how I always visualised meeting you after she died?’ Joel says, and John looks at him.

‘I always visualised punching you,’ Joel says and laughs. John, too laughs.

‘I deserve it. If it satisfies your anger and rids me of all the crimes I had committed, then go ahead,’ John says, closing his eyes.

‘She wouldn’t want me to do that to you. Not after you have finally found your calling,’ Joel says, smiling. His eyes were moist.

‘She was fond of your voice. She would be happy up there listening to you sing now,’ Joel says, and John looks at him with moist eyes.

They sit there chatting and reminiscing about the old days for a while.

‘You know she was always upset with Samuel and me because we would sit here till late night,’ John says, looking at the porch.

‘Samuel would not let me go to bed without listening to me singing. He said my voice was like a lullaby for him. I would sing, and we would drink for hours sitting on these very steps,’ he says, laughing as Joel looks on.

‘And then Samuel and I…’ he says and pauses.

‘… and then you guys made some shitty choices,’ Joel says, shaking his head.

‘Well, I guess we can’t turn the time back, so we all gotta move ahead, and after you left that day, I thought hard. I acted badly that day, so please accept my sincere apologies,’ Joel says, and John is astonished.

‘You are sorry?’ John is surprised.

‘I am the one who must apologise to you and Mrs Russo,’ John says, and Joel stops him.

‘What has happened can’t be changed, John. What matters is that you have made good use of your second chance,’ Joel says, smiling. He extends his hand towards John. John looks at his hand in disbelief and shakes his hand.

‘You have no idea what this means to me,’ John says with moist eyes.

‘Come inside, let's have a beer,’ Joel says.

‘Why don’t we have it here,’ John says, looking around. Joel brings a few pints.

Joel raises a toast, ‘To second chances in life.’ John brings his bottle close and clinks with Joel’s bottle. ‘To second chances,’ he says.

Sylvia smiles as she sees John walking out of the street with a broad smile on his face.

‘I can’t believe it,’ John says ecstatically.

‘You better believe it, baby. You are on a roll,’ Sylvia says as they drive towards John’s apartment.

*****

John and Sylvia get married a month later, in the presence of their family and friends. Joel, Clyde & his mother and Thomas and his family also grace the wedding event. It was a small gathering of close friends and family.

*****

John’s company became successful, and he was living a respectable life. Solomon and Pauline were partners in the company, and they, too, lived a happy life.

John had got the second chance he was seeking so badly after getting out of prison. He made the most by helping others. While his recording company gave ex-cons & many new singers and artists a chance, he had also set up a charity where he provided homes and food for the homeless. He also offered free medicines to the needy at many hospitals across Canada.

The name John Sweets Russo was once again synonymous with everyone, but this time it was for all the right reasons.

John didn’t stop singing even after age made it difficult for him to sing continuously. He had reduced live shows, but he kept recording songs. Notwithstanding age, he still sang with the same zeal.

He also appeared as a Guest Judge on ‘Canadian Talent’ multiple times.

FULFILLMENT

John was feeling restless for some time. He was taking frequent breaks and seemed quite tired as well. 'Are you alright, John?' Pauline asks as she sees John gasping for breath backstage.

'I am alright, don't worry. I am just out of breath,' John says, smiling. He walks towards the stage entrance.

'You don't have to do this, John. We can always cancel the gig,' Pauline says, looking concerned for John's health. This was the first time she had seen John like this.

'You are not getting any younger; you have to rest,' Pauline says as John throws an air kiss towards her walking on the stage. John and the band were performing at a sold-out event at the MTelus Arena in Montreal.

Pauline was concerned, and she shared about John's health with Sylvia, who flew to Montreal immediately. Sylvia was adamant, and John had to relent and fly back to Toronto with her along with Pauline and the rest of the band. Sylvia had cancelled all their gigs for the next week, insisting that John must rest at home.

Although John was reluctant, Sylvia gets him to a hospital for a thorough check-up by a doctor. Sylvia didn't want to take any chance with John's health.

John changes back into his clothes after a thorough check-up by the doctor.

'Looks like a case of old age,' the doctor said and giggled as he sat in front of Sylvia and John. John looks at the doctor with utter indifference, and the doctor stops laughing.

The doctor clears his throat and continues, 'Everything seems to be in the order. He just needs to rest for a few days.'

'Told you,' John says, looking at Sylvia and gets up to leave the room.

‘Ahhh…’ it was just this single syllable sound from the doctor’s vocal cords. John stops and turns around.

The doctor was holding a notepad and pen.

John smiles and gets down to give his autograph.

‘Can you please make it out to Lucy?’ the doctor says with a puppy face. He points towards a photo of Lucy and him on his table. John gladly accedes and writes, ‘To Lucy with love from Gangsta Grooves,’ and inscribed his signature underneath. He leaves as the doctor admires the page with the message and John’s autograph.

‘She’s beautiful,’ Sylvia says. ‘Thank you!’ the doctor says, blushing.

‘Are you sure he’s alright?’ Sylvia asks the doctor.

‘Look, he has to remember that he’s getting old. He needs to take it slow,’ the doctor says. Sylvia smiles but knows that it would be a herculean task to stop John from performing. She comes out of the doctor’s room and finds John munching on candies at the reception. Sylvia and John take the lift to the basement where their car was parked.

‘Told you, it’s a waste of time,’ John says as Sylvia and he gets into the car. John sounded like a child who hated going to a doctor.

‘He has asked you to rest, PERIOD,’ Sylvia says, raising her voice. John was clearly annoyed, but he complies.

John wanted to get back into action quickly, but he relents as he was also worried about Sylvia getting annoyed. He spends the next few days at home. Sylvia had rented a flat on King St West near Lake Ontario. They would together go for walks around the lake and spend time at home playing the piano. He took the piano everywhere he went.

He should have gotten better, but something was amiss.

*****

‘I miss you guys so much,’ John says as he looks at his parent’s photo.

‘What's wrong?’ Sylvia asks, seeing John talking to himself.

‘Nothing's wrong; just missing them,’ John says, taking a deep breath.

‘You are right; I need to rest. I am feeling tired,’ he says, sitting on the recliner. He watches the beautiful view from his room balcony. Lake Ontario is visible as he looks out. Sylvia sits beside him, kisses him on his forehead, and holds on to him tightly.

‘Never seen you like this. Whatever happened to the stubborn old John?’ Sylvia says, smiling.

‘I was going out to buy some groceries, but I will be with you,’ she says.

‘No, go, please. I am all right. Let’s go for a walk afterwards,’ John says, kissing her and Sylvia leaves.

John gets up and looks at his mother’s diary placed on a table below the photos on the wall. Though he had kept it with him, he could never muster enough courage to read it.

‘I am sorry,’ he said, looking at the photos and picking up the diary.

John holds on to the diary while looking out for a while and then flips through the pages reading the last few entries.

‘Today, Jasmeet and Harinder argued, and Jasmeet left angrily. I waited for him till late at night, but he never returned. May Waheguru bless him.’

‘It’s been two days, and Jasmeet hasn’t returned. Harinder enquired with his friends in the neighbourhood, and even they didn't know his whereabouts. Jarnail, a cop from the neighbourhood, said Jasmeet’s an adult, and they won’t register a missing person’s complaint unless there is probable cause. We must give him some privacy is what we have been told by many. But, he’s our son…’ was another entry.

‘It’s been an entire month, and Jasmeet hasn’t returned. I am worried about him. I know he misses Jasmeet, but Harinder doesn’t talk about it…’ This entry had some distorted words. Seemed as if tears were raining when this entry was made. John closes the diary. He couldn't garner the courage to continue reading further. John suddenly feels a searing pain and holds the left side of his chest. He looks around, sweating and then closes his eyes, resting his head on the recliner.

'MAA,' he cries as the pain worsens.

'Jasmeet,' is what he hears suddenly, and tears curl down his cheeks. It was his mother's voice.

He slowly opens his eyes and is amazed to see his mother and father standing in front of him. They both were smiling.

'I must be dreaming,' John mumbles as his mother stretches her arm towards him.

'You are not dreaming, son,' she said. Her voice was as calm and soothing as the pleasant breeze.

John smiles and reaches out with a trembling hand and holds her hand. John stands up. He is ecstatic to see them in person.

'I am sorry mom, dad,' he said, looking at both with folded hands.

'You can stop feeling guilty, son. Life was meant to be the way it turned out for all of us. What matters is that you came back,' his father said smiling, and John nodded.

Sylvia comes back after some time, along with Solomon and Cindy. She called them to help cheer up John.

'What's up, Sweets?' Solomon exclaims, walking into the living room, but John remains silent. He is still sitting on the recliner, looking out of the balcony. The window is wide open, and the curtains are flying around due to the wind. They look like the wings of an angel.

'What's wrong?' Sylvia asks, seeing Solomon stand there like a statue.

'I think he's asleep,' Solomon says. Sylvia walks up to the recliner quietly to check on John. She stands in front of John and looks at his face.

John's eyes are closed, and his head is resting on the recliner. The expression on his face is peaceful, and he has his mother's diary in his hand. Solomon rushes as Sylvia's eyes are moist. Solomon looks at John, and even he is teary-eyed. Sylvia removes the journal from under his hand and looks at the page. John had kept the quote from Guru Granth Sahib in the diary and was reading it before his eyes closed.

Cindy walks in, seeing Solomon and Sylvia in tears. She looks at John.

'He's finally with them now,' she says, and they all look at his parent's photo on the wall.

*****

John was eighty one when he died. Celebrities and fans from across the world mourned his death, and a memorial was erected in a park in the St James Town neighbourhood to commemorate Jasmeet John Sweets Russo's memory.

His charities continued to help the needy, and Langars (Community kitchen of a gurdwara, which serves meals to all free of charge and does not distinguish religion, caste, gender, economic status, or ethnicity) was organised by Sylvia in many Gurdwaras around Toronto. John's music label kept his vision alive by giving many new singers and artists a chance to launch their career.

John was cremated as per Sikh customs in Meadowvale Funeral Centre, Brampton and his ashes were immersed in Lakes across Canada.

It didn't matter if he died as Jasmeet Singh Brar or John Sweets Russo, but what mattered was that he died being himself and not pretending to be someone else. He died feeling comfortable about his identity. He made the most of his second chance with his name immortalised as a true Canadian.

JASVEER

Life is all about choices, so you can always choose between ice hockey or cricket, NHL or IPL, Virat Kohli of Royal Challengers Bangalore, or Auston Matthews of Toronto Maple Leafs. We all make choices; what matters is that we are comfortable about our choices so that we don't have to hide them from the world. Ultimately it is all about choices we make and never make choices just to fit in. Be comfortable with your heritage and yourself. Don't ever change yourself or your appearance to look like someone else.

It really doesn't matter which country you live in; what matters is that you respect the law of the land, culture, and language without losing your own essence. Every culture offers both good and bad things, and it's our choice what we want to accept.

Doesn't matter what your religion or ethnicity is; God created us equal and gave us unique features and characteristics which forms our identity. You must firstly be comfortable with your identity. If you are not satisfied with your own identity, whichever identity you adopt will never do justice to your personality.

To all the bullies: The more you disrespect and compete with people from other cultures and religions, the more you lose a bit of yourself. Compete with yourself and become a better human being rather than constantly trying to prove that you are superior to others. Don't ever look down or disrespect someone else's religion, culture, or heritage.

I am not a preacher trying to preach the wisdom of becoming a good Canadian citizen. I am new here and lost myself. I am also looking for my calling, but I am comfortable with who I am, and I am willing to learn and adapt. Above all, I am confident about my choices, and I am willing to stand by them.

Cheers, everyone, and thank you for taking time out to read…

The Incredible Mr Sweets

*****

REVIEW OF JASVEER'S WORK

SHAHENSHAH – STORY OF SHRENIK SHAH, THE CANCER CONQUEROR

Available on: eBook - Amazon Kindle, Google Playstore, Kobo. Paperback - Evincepub.com, Amazon (Worldwide), Flipkart

Dr Siddharth Shah 5.0 out of 5 stars - Zeal for the will of life: Shrenik bhai is a very energetic person. If you don't know about him, you can never believe he's a near silver jubilee cancer survivor. Pleasure and privileged to have known him. He's a great person. The books she's you through the journey of an unbeaten desire for the quest of life. Recommended for someone who feels low morally and weak mentally.

Gobind Prasad rated it 5 out of 5 stars on Amazon - I liked this book. People who are interested in an overview of the glorious life of Shrenik Shah, a cancer survivor and a cancer conqueror will most probably be interested in reading this book. One of the things that were especially interesting was that there were many different colors, flavors, and fragrances in life. Also, there was a big contrast between the normal person and the cancer patient. This book was very well written and suitable for all ages.

Nitin Gupta 5.0 out of 5 stars on Amazon - Highly recommended.

Books and More rated 5.0 out of 5 stars on Amazon - Amazing book: Written and narrated by Jasveer Singh Dangi, ShahenShah tells the story of Shrenik Shah; a cancer survivor. Cancer is one of the deadliest diseases, and the author has done his absolute best in narrating the story of the highly energetic cancer survivor, Shrenik. . As the author points out in the blurb - "Shrenik Shah, being a humble and kind man that he is, wanted a simple name for his life story but I convinced him to go with this name because I think not all ShehanShah's wear crown and command riches, some like Shrenik Shah are ShehanShah because they conquered their greatest adversary with brevity and true grit.' This quality of our protagonist is truly mirrored in the book. The book is heart touching, and soulful, and keeps you hooked till the end. The narration, the cover, and the ever so apt title are top notch. Totally Recommended.

THE METRO-MANIAC CHRONICLES

Kanwarpal Singh rated it 5 out of 5 stars on Amazon - My review: This book is very simple and easy to read. The book is small and can be read quickly and the language is too simple as well. While reading this book I felt like I was talking to someone who is my co-passenger and sharing all his experiences in a very friendly and humorous way. The book has 30 contents and each content has a different topic named to it and each content is barely two to three pages. I really like how the author observes all the small details of his daily journey. I like: 1. The title of each content 2. Lucid and easy language 3. The honesty of the author's writing. After reading the book I got a feel for traveling the metro and to find all those experiences on my own. I like the book.

Gopal R N rated it 5 out of 5 stars on Amazon - Delhi metro is a great way to travel around the city. We all know that Delhi is a very big and crowded place and that is why the roads of Delhi are full of traffic every time, and Delhi metro is a mean by which we can travel around the city at a very less cost, and it consumes lesser time than traveling by a motorbike or car. Other countries call it trams, in India, Metro trains are the name of such a great traveling option. Author Jasveer Singh has penned down a book by observing various kinds of people who are usually found in Delhi Metro. Through his Writing, Author proves to be an observing person and has a good balance of sarcasm with sense of humor. Metro Maniac is a very short read which differentiate people into 30 different categories, and it is fun to read about them. Whatever the Author have written, it is totally acceptable and relate to large audience especially from Delhi. I think I belong to "The BookLovers Club" and partially to "Sombie" Category and it was funny to read. The language is easy. One can pick this book while travelling in Metro and can relate it on spot and I am sure readers will smile after finishing each chapter. The Book Cover is designed too beautiful. I strongly recommend this book to every person.

The Write House (@bhairavireads on Facebook) - The Metro-Maniac Chronicles : Through the eyes of an Obsessive-Compulsive Metro Maniac written by Jasveer Singh Dangi is a mini-book describing different kinds of Delhi Metro travellers. The author has made various categories of types of people he observed while travelling in the Delhi Metro. This book has a unique concept as reading about every single one is interesting. It consists of categories like the cool ones, the lecturer, dreamers, i don't give a duck (which refer to those ruthless people who just have a stone- cold expression on their face) and yes, the booklover's club. The author has given a total of thirty types and each one was fascinating to read. The language of the book is easy and very easy to read. It can be finished within thirty minutes. I think among all the categories, I liked dreamers most and of course book lovers. People who never observe while travelling in the metro will start thinking about all these categories. I recommend it to those who want a light read. This would be perfect to have little entertainment in just a small amount of time.

DOUBLE ONE ZERO (110) – OUT OF THE SHADOWS
Available on: Amazon Kindle & Google Books (eBook), Notionpress.com, Amazon.in

Amazon user rated it 4 out of 5 stars on Amazon - This book is about an intelligence security agent who met with an accident and lost his memory but with a name slip in his pocket, the whole story have many twists that came at appropriate time and the characters are well balanced and placed that they did a fabulous job with it and most of them have a mask on their face , and it's a story of country love, security forces, mafia group of security forces, their heads how they were taken down , the author did a fabulous writing and if ever this book is made into a movie it will be blockbuster. I really like the title. At first I thought it would be a story of some failed mission but the writer makes it clear in the starting the meaning of the title and this novel has the power and every reader out there must read this thriller novel.

Priya Agarwal rated 5 out of 5 stars on Goodreads - The story is about an intelligent security agent Amandeep who unfortunately lost his memory. Amandeep must find out for himself or to recall his memory. It is a lengthy read. Narration is quite different and difficult. Book is good at first and grows very interesting as we read further. Action scenes were described so amazingly that it was like watching a movie. At first, I was confused about the name and the cover but after reading the book I can say that it is perfect. Cover is good. Readers will feel a lot of thrilling experience and enjoy reading the book. I enjoyed the end of the book. It was quite expected, and it was superb. Recommendations yes.

Night Reader rated it 5 out of 5 on Goodreads - Written like a script I would love it if this book is adapted into a movie. The chase, the characters, and the story line couldn't have been more exciting. The detailing. Man, the author really put their heart and soul in the book. The story of 110 is so engaging that I could not keep it down at all. I can't reveal anything about the book because at every step there is a revelation you did not expect. My first spy thriller of 2020 couldn't have been better.

DIARY FROM HEAVEN

Available on: Amazon Kindle (eBook), Notionpress.com, Amazon.in **Mohan Sharma rated 4 out of 5 stars on Amazon** - The author has wonderfully expressed the words and has beautifully scripted the book. This book contains 14 different chapters, where the main character named Arun has confessed his life. To match the fast-moving world, he opted for the drug and ruined his life but somehow, he managed to overcome it. He has confessed every single part of life through different chapters in this book. It is a wonderful book to read. You must read this.

Sameeksha rated 4 out of 5 stars on Amazon - The book consists of 14 chapters which describe Arun's different phases and struggles in life. Things I liked: 1. The title is catchy. 2. The cover is alluring. 3. The language is simple and easy. 4. The narration is amazing. 5. The storyline is intriguing. 6. Overall a nice enjoyable read.

Tanishka Tiwari rated 5 out of 5 stars on Amazon - This book is an epitome of real-life struggle that one goes through every day. Hiding is always easy, but confessing is something that needs a lot of courage. The characters of Arun confess his life struggles and failures in this book. The book summarizes beautiful thoughts which everyone must apply in their daily life. Language of the book is quite simple. Narration is beautiful! Personally, I loved this book.

VERSION ONE AND A HALF (VERSION 1 ½)

Available on: Amazon Kindle (eBook), Notionpress.com

Ravneet Kaur rated 5 out of 5 stars on Amazon.in - One of the best books I have ever read...!! Reviewed in India on 6 December 2018 Format: The book reminds you of the late '80s. How the lifestyle was completely different from that of today. It makes me realize that being a kid of today's generation is not actually fun if compared to a kid of the '80s. The trend of outdoor games has just disappeared. The book will give you a tour of the '80s and will remind you what lifestyle actually is. The book is completely worth reading. The writer has really put a lot of effort into penning down his experiences of being a kid of the late '80s.

Aditya rated 5 out of 5 stars on Goodreads - Read this within 2 days. This book is an absolute blessing and one can redefine their way of tackling difficult situations by reading this book. Just awesome. Jasveer ji you are amazing through this you can change the life of people.

Rahul Asati rated 5 out of 5 stars on Goodreads - This is the best book I ever read before feeling matching circumstances in my life too. He wrote very well that u will complete this book in one stroke. Language is too easy to understand. Thank you, author, for such a beautiful and inspiring book.

Khushi rated 5 out of 5 stars on Goodreads - Occasionally, every person needs some mental support to keep on going despite failures and depression. This is a book worth keeping by your side and give a read whenever you feel down or demotivated.

CPSIA information can be obtained
at www.ICGtesting.com
Printed in the USA
LVHW111954220621
690868LV00005B/235

9 781777 725334